Y0-BST-401

The men and women who fought each other at Fort Starvation . . .

JOHN SLATER was out for revenge—he didn't mind being called a killer.

COLONEL ORPINGTON had failed at everything—even the army.

JIM BONNIWELL was a self-acclaimed killer. He had sworn to get Slater.

SUSAN ORPINGTON might have been willing to give up the money . . . but then she learned what Slater really wanted.

Bantam Books by Frank Gruber
Ask your bookseller for the books you have missed

FORT STARVATION
OUTLAW
THIS GUN IS STILL

Fort Starvation

by Frank Gruber

BANTAM BOOKS
TORONTO · NEW YORK · LONDON

This low-priced Bantam Book
has been completely reset in a type face
designed for easy reading, and was printed
from new plates. It contains the complete
text of the original hard-cover edition.
NOT ONE WORD HAS BEEN OMITTED.

FORT STARVATION

A Bantam Book / published by arrangement with
the Estate of the author

PRINTING HISTORY

Holt Rinehart edition published February 1953
Serialization appeared in RANCH ROMANCES MAGAZINE
Bantam Pennant edition / April 1954
New Bantam edition / September 1970
2nd printing .... March 1975   3rd printing ...... August 1980

All rights reserved.
Copyright 1952, 1953 by Frank Gruber.
This book may not be reproduced in whole or in part, by
mimeograph or any other means, without permission.
For information address: Bantam Books, Inc.

ISBN 0-553-14180-5

Published simultaneously in the United States and Canada

Bantam Books are published by Bantam Books, Inc. Its trade-
mark, consisting of the words "Bantam Books" and the por-
trayal of a bantam, is Registered in U.S. Patent and Trademark
Office and in other countries. Marca Registrada. Bantam
Books, Inc., 666 Fifth Avenue, New York, New York 10103.

PRINTED IN CANADA

COVER PRINTED IN U.S.A.

12 11 10 9 8 7 6 5 4 3

1

In the spring of 1861, a detachment of the Third U.S. Cavalry, forced by the spring floods to make a detour, entered a land-locked valley in Utah and came upon the charred ruins of a small stockade. Signs of violence, which had withstood the burning, were apparent and the soldiers made an examination, a hasty one, for the result was gruesome. Emaciated, mutilated corpses were scattered about.

The soldiers removed what identification they could find, buried the remains of the bodies in a single grave and quickly left the scene.

First Lieutenant Alfred Orpington, the officer in charge of the detachment, made his report to regimental headquarters—and soon ugly rumors spread about the tragedy at "Fort Starvation."

Indians had besieged the stockade, starved the defenders and burned the place in the end. But had the Indians mutilated the bodies, or . . .?

Lawrence, Kansas, had suffered during the war. The scars left by the murderous Quantrill during his abortive raid in '63 were still in evidence. But the house before which Slater stood had not been injured by the war. Only nature had hurt it. Nature—and human neglect. The wind and snow and rain had peeled and stripped off the paint. Neglect by its owner had caused the rest. A freshly painted sign nailed to the gatepost read: *Col. Alfred Orpington, U.S.A. Retired.*

Slater swung open the sagging gate and strode up a weed-grown path to the door of the house. He knocked. There was movement inside the house but no one came to the door.

He knocked again, louder. After a long wait the door was finally opened two or three inches. A half-grown girl with a smudged face and her hair in pigtails peered through the slot.

"I'd like to see Colonel Orpington," Slater said.

"He isn't here."

"Do you know where I can find him? I've come a long way."

The girl hesitated, frowning. She was conscious of her soiled house dress, although probably not aware that her face was dirty.

She said, "You might try the Wheat Exchange. It's a—a saloon."

"Thank you."

Slater turned away. At the gate he looked back. She was still watching him from the house, the door now opened a little wider.

The Wheat Growers' Exchange was a half block from the Eldridge House, during the border wars "the biggest hotel west of Chicago." It was a large saloon, well patronized for the time of the day.

Slater ordered a glass of beer and as he quaffed the cooling stuff sized up the various customers at the bar.

He spotted Colonel Orpington almost immediately. Except that he was several inches taller, he bore an amazing likeness to U. S. Grant, even to the weathered, open uniform coat that dangled almost to his knees. And the bloated, dissipated features.

Slater carried his glass of beer down the bar and stopped beside the colonel. "Colonel Orpington, I believe."

Colonel Orpington regarded Slater without enthusiasm, without disfavor. "That depends. If you're a bill collector, my name isn't Orpington."

"Your daughter told me I might find you here," Slater said, and saw the least flicker of a gleam come into the other man's eyes. "My name is Slater, John Slater. I might add that I also wore a uniform of that color."

"Who didn't?" said the colonel sourly. "And you probably

2

wore shoulder straps, too. Captains, majors and colonels will be ten cents a hundredweight for the next fifty years." Orpington made an impatient, brushing gesture. Then he suddenly looked sharply, thoughtfully, at Slater.

"Slater, you said?"

"That's right. Ever hear the name before?"

"I had a thousand men in my regiment. I'm sure two or three were called Slater."

"Possibly. I thought you might have remembered the name from somewhere else."

"Where?"

Slater took another draught of his beer and signaled to the bartender to refill his glass. He also indicated the colonel's. When the man got the glasses, Slater look at the colonel and said, "Fort Starvation."

Colonel Orpington was silent for a long moment and it seemed to Slater that a curtain came down over the other man's eyes. Then at last Orpington let out a slow, almost imperceptible sigh.

"Fort Starvation," he said. "That was a hundred years ago."

"Nine years," Slater corrected. "My father was Paul Slater."

"I was a first lieutenant," Orpington mused aloud. "Yes, I know. I look fifty, but I'm forty-four. I was in the class of '48 and in '61 I was still a first lieutenant." His eyes became vague again. "I was six years ahead of Jeb Stuart. Phil Sheridan was behind me. Custer was still a schoolboy when I graduated from the Point."

"Maybe they got the breaks."

"I wound up a brevet colonel," Orpington went on tonelessly. "A brevet colonel, but still only a captain in the regular army."

The bartender brought the fresh glasses of beer, set them down on the bar. Slater put a quarter on the mahogany and signaled with his head to a table near by.

"Shall we sit down?"

Colonel Orpington sighed, picked up his beer and moved to the table. Slater followed. They seated themselves and Orpington leaned back in his chair and thrust his legs out before him. He drank some of his beer and stared at the floor.

"You were in command of the detachment that found Fort Starvation," Slater prodded.

Slowly Orpington roused himself from his bitter memories. "You say your father was there?"

Slater's jaw tightened a little. "Don't you *know?*"

Orpington shrugged. "They were all dead."

"I read the report you made out."

"Oh, so that's how you got my name." Orpington nodded. "Some things happened in '61. Sumter, Bull Run. That little affair out in Utah . . ." Then he realized that it wouldn't be so trivial to the son of one of the victims. "Your father, eh? Sorry. It wasn't pretty. But you've seen dead men."

"I was at Gettysburg. And a few other places."

It took more than an hour for Slater to get the whole story, an hour of prodding and getting the man back from commentaries on human frailties. And five glasses of beer. Stripped of verbiage and nonessentials, Colonel Orpington's story was one of stark horror.

2

"There never was a Fort Starvation," Colonel Orpington said. "It was a cabin with a stockade around it that enclosed a spring. What they were doing there, why they built the cabin and the stockade, no one knows. Unless . . ." Orpington looked inquiringly at Slater. The latter shook his head.

"Indians? The Piutes were a cowardly lot, as a rule. The Mormons, well, you know about Mountain Meadows. The Avenging Angels were rough customers. That's why we were out there, of course. The Mormons were in full rebellion, slaughtering immigrants who tried to cross Utah. Colonel Johnston, ah, if he hadn't fallen at Shiloh—yes, General Albert Sidney Johnston—you'd have really heard of him. All right, all that's beside the point. What I'm trying to bring out is that it's my guess the fort was built to stand off Mormons, not Indians. But it was Indians who got them."

"How do you know?" Slater interrupted.

"I had seven years on the plains and in the mountains. I know Indians. They always carry off their dead, but there were plenty of arrows, broken spears and lances all around. Take my word, it was Indians. And it was a long siege. They had plenty of water from the spring inside the stockade, but food—well, five men can eat a lot."

"Five men?" said Slater. "There were six."

Orpington looked sharply at Slater. "We buried five."

"Are you *sure?*"

"The bodies were mutilated, everybody knows that, but . . ." Orpington frowned as the memory of it came back to him. "They weren't mutilated *that* much. . . ."

"Say it," Slater said bluntly. "They turned cannibal."

"It's not without precedent," Orpington said severely. "Almost forty members of the Donner party were eaten by the others, back in '46 and '47. And in Colorado——"

"I want to know the details of Fort Starvation," Slater said, bringing Orpington back to the main topic. "You found identification on the various bodies . . ."

"If you've read my report, you should know that I stated very clearly that the Indians had gone over the corpses. Naturally they took whatever attracts the fancy of a stupid savage. Rings, trinkets, watches. Letters and things like that they ignored."

"You turned everything in to Headquarters at Fort Ogden?"

"Everything." The Colonel hesitated, then repeated firmly, "Everything."

"You missed something."

"What?"

Slater studied the drink-besotted retired Army officer a moment. Then he reached into his coat and brought out a small flat parcel wrapped in oilskin. He unfolded the oilskin and exposed several articles.

"You've seen these before?"

Orpington regarded the objects unblinkingly. "Slater," he said, "you read my report. We buried five bodies, all more or less mutilated. I don't want to go into the details. For that matter, I couldn't if I wanted. I—I don't remember. My men did the actual searching of the bodies and the burying. And they did it in one hell of a hurry. Try to understand; none of *their* relatives were there. It was a dirty job and they wanted to get it over with as soon as possible."

"I understand all that. But since one of the men *was* my father, I want the details."

"But I don't know them. I was an officer, in command of the detachment. The men did the actual work. They searched the bodies and brought me their findings."

Slater picked up an old-fashioned, faded tintype. "Do you remember *this?*"

Orpington reached out, hesitated with his hand in mid-air,

then grimacing a little, took the tintype. He looked at it. "Yes, I remember it. A very handsome woman. . . ."

"My mother."

"I'm sorry."

"She died when I was twelve."

Orpington turned the tintype over. "There's no name on it. I remember now, there were a number of objects with no identification. We just wrapped them all up and . . ."

Slater held up a moldy leather purse, which was closed with a buckskin drawstring. Some coins clinked inside it. "You remember this?"

"Yes. It contained two twenty-dollar gold pieces." Orpington's eyes brightened. "That was one of the arguments for Indians. White men would have taken the money." Then he winced a little. "The money's still in it."

"I didn't need it." Slater pawed over some of the articles and held up an envelope. Orpington leaned forward to read the inscription on it.

"Oh yes, a letter addressed to Slater at Salt Lake."

"From me."

Orpington nodded, then looked sharply at Slater. "It comes back now. You're the Harvard man. Or was it Yale? I remember now we thought it odd the son of a trapper in the Rockies attending one of the big eastern colleges."

"What makes you think my father was a trapper?"

"What else would they have been doing in those mountains?"

Slater did not answer that. He picked up a short ivory comb. Orpington looked at it and shook his head. Slater held up the last object from the oilskin packet, a small leather-bound booklet. Orpington looked at it, puzzled. "What's that?"

"My father's diary."

"But there wasn't any diary!" exclaimed Orpington.

"How do you know? You don't remember!"

"I'd remember a thing like that. We—we read every scrap of writing, all the letters . . ."

Slater dropped the booklet and whipped up the letter. "This one, too?"

"Of course. How else would I have known that you were in college at the time?"

"You remembered *that*, but you didn't know whether it

was Harvard or Yale." Slater made an impatient gesture. "All right, that wouldn't count with someone not definitely interested. A West Pointer. But—you said my father was a trapper. In this letter I refer to his prospecting . . . not trapping."

"Trapping, prospecting, what's the difference?"

"A lot."

Slater glowered at Orpington. The latter scowled. "What's the game, Slater?"

"There isn't any."

"That diary . . . it wasn't at Fort Starvation."

Slater gathered up the various objects, started folding them back into the oilskin.

"As you said, it was a dirty job. You got it over with as quickly as possible. Nobody could blame you for that."

"There wasn't any book like that."

"And you weren't interested——"

"I'd have been interested in the diary. And I didn't say *I* wasn't interested. My men, no. But—this was the spring of '61. Before I even heard about Sumter."

"The Pony Express was running in '61."

Orpington leaned back in his chair. He toyed with his emptied beer glass. Then suddenly he picked up the glass and banged it smartly on the table.

"Now, look here, Slater, I don't think I care for your attitude. You're as good as accusing me——"

"Of what?"

"I don't know. But that book—that's a trick. There wasn't any diary."

"All right, there wasn't."

"Then what's the game? What're you trying to prove?"

"You buried five bodies. But there were six men at Fort Starvation."

For just a moment the significance of Slater's statement made no impression on Orpington, but then he suddenly reacted violently.

"There couldn't have been!"

"Why not?"

"The Indians——"

"One of them could have escaped. Or made a deal with the Indians."

"Or been taken a prisoner!" Orpington scowled heavily.

"*If* there *were* six."

"There were. My father wrote me in November, '60."

Orpington blinked owlishly. "The postman picked up the letter at Fort Starvation, I suppose?"

Slater ignored the other's sarcasm. "They built the fort, intending to winter there. My father went in to Salt Lake for supplies, before the big snows. He picked up my letter there and wrote me. He said he was going to spend the winter in the mountains with *five* men——"

"Did he name the men?"

Slater shook his head. Orpington's pouted lips moved in and out. "That's no proof, Slater. There *could* have been six men in the fall. But one of them could have changed his mind about wintering in the mountains. Or—one *could* have died during the winter. The Indian attack wasn't until April."

"And one of them *could* have betrayed the others to the Indians," Slater said evenly. "For the sixty thousand dollars in gold that they had already dug in '60."

Orpington stared at Slater a moment, then he whistled softly.

3

At the little Mormon settlement on the western side of the mountain they told Slater nothing about Fort Starvation. He asked, but only one man would even admit that he had ever heard of it. The others merely shook their heads and turned their backs on him. They didn't like Gentiles anyway. But they sold him some things: food, a pack horse, a shovel, a pick.

It was in the center of a landlocked valley. Except for the ruins, the valley looked as if it had never been visited by white men. Yet, as Slater rode up his nostrils caught the faint smell of—not smoke, but charred wood; wood that had been fire not too long ago.

He loosened the Navy Colt in his holster, touched the butt of the rifle in the saddle scabbard and dismounted at some distance from the ruins.

He slipped the rifle out of the sheath and stood for minutes, while his eyes searched the ruins, the high grass, the rocks some distance beyond and to the left. Then, a light frown creasing his forehead, he advanced to the fort.

The stockade gate was down, partly burned. One side of the stockade was completely burned. The other three sides stood, but showed the ravages of fire. Originally the stockade had been some thirty by forty feet, enclosing a spring within the walls and the cabin, which had been not more than twelve by eighteen feet. A one-room cabin, quite large enough for five—or six—prospectors.

Slater stood outside the fallen gate for a moment, listening. A pack rat scurried inside, but Slater knew the sound for what it was and was not alarmed. In fact, the noise reassured him and he entered the stockade.

A small hillock, grass-covered, just inside the gate, caught his eyes. It was seven or eight feet wide and about the same in length, perhaps a little longer. It was a man-made mound.

Fire had gutted the cabin from the inside. Very little of it was left; charred ends of logs, one corner fallen, but not burned as much as the rest. That was all. But Slater circled the ruins carefully and when he got to the far side pushed a couple of logs together and, stepping up on them, peered out over the remains of the stockade wall. He searched the far end of the valley.

After a while he stepped down, left the stockade and circled it. The smell of charred logs was stronger again in his nostrils. It could not be from the long-burned cabin and stockade. He returned to his horses, led the pack animal to the walls and tied it to a log. Then he mounted his saddle horse and made two complete circuits of the stockade, the first one fifty yards from the logs, the second a hundred. Near the rocks on the south side of the valley he found the remains of the fire.

Dismounting, he felt the ashes. They were cold, but not too cold when he dug down into them. There had been fire here as recently as yesterday.

Boot tracks. Hoofprints. One man, one horse. They had been here one day, perhaps two days, but only one night. A large fire.

The man had braved the valley, but the night had bothered him. Ghosts of men, men who had died the most horrible of human deaths.

A hundred yards from the mound that buried the mortal remains, but too close—at night. A man who had nerved himself to enter the valley and spend a night here because he sought something.

Slater returned to the fort, unsaddled his horse and turned it loose to graze. The pack horse, however, he kept tied to the log. He was not too sure of it. He took down the

11

shovel from the pack and reentered the stockade. The mound was untouched. Whoever had been here the day before had felt that there was no use digging into it.

But Slater had to know. He had to know everything, no matter how trivial. He had lost his nerves at the second battle of Bull Run, but there was a fine film of perspiration on his forehead before he had dug for more than a minute.

The soldiers under command of First Lieutenant Alfred Orpington had been in a hurry back in '61. The grave was a shallow one, not more than two feet deep. Slater had it open in less than an hour. He spent two hours more removing bones . . . then he dug some more just to be certain nothing was underneath. And at last, as the sun was going over the mountains in the west, he refilled the grave.

Five bodies had been buried here in '61. Slater had verified that.

He left the stockade and looked toward the rocks a hundred yards away. Since someone had camped there not very long ago, it would prove suitable for another encampment. Wood was not too far away if he wanted a fire.

But there was wood closer. Right here, beside him. He started to gather charred log ends for a fire just outside the stockade, then, suddenly angry, carried the logs inside. He threw away the big pieces and made a fire only large enough to cook his bacon. And when he had eaten he let the fire go out.

He put the pack horse on a long rope, carried a blanket inside the fort, and rolled himself up in it.

His saddle horse whickered once during the night. Slater got up and made a circle of the area surrounding Fort Starvation. His horse trotted beside him part of the way, then left him and joined the pack horse.

Slater went back to his blanket and remained awake until dawn. He ate a cold breakfast, then began a methodical search of the ruins.

First the strip of ground inside what had been the walls and outside the cabin. He combed the ground thoroughly and found many things left there by the occupants, before and during the siege. But nothing of importance. Two rusted hunting knives, the stock of a rifle, a badly corroded Navy Colt revolver. All junk. The arrowheads, pieces of arrow shafts, he did not even bother to pick up. There were too many.

Then he attacked the remains of the cabin. Piece by piece he picked up the charred pieces of logs, examined them and tossed them aside onto a pile. There weren't too many, but he took his time and by midday reached the logs of the corner that still remained, after the final burning and the weight of the years of snows.

There was nothing in the logs except an arrowhead or two, a chunk of lead, proving that at least one of the Indians had been armed with a rifle. Underneath the logs, however, he found the remains of a double-deck bunk. On it were molded bits of blanket, a grass-filled mattress that crumpled to his touch and from which a pack rat scurried.

The remnants of a pair of trousers, one pocket containing a small chunk of gold-flecked quartz and the stub of a lead pencil. Under the bunk what was left of a pair of boots after the pack rats had chewed away practically all of the uppers.

And then, on two logs just above the level of the lower bunk, he found the carvings. A man had lain here on the bunk and had turned to the wall and with a knife had recorded the last hours, days, of his life, cutting into the wood of the cabin wall.

One wall had eighteen notches cut into it, one for each day. And in the log beside the noched one, a scant half-dozen abbreviated lines.

```
12 day
Inds closing
13 day
Laik wound
14 day
Bonn died
```

No more after that. But there were eighteen notches in the log beside the carved diary. The carver had lived another four days. He had probably been too weak by then to carve more than the daily notches . . . if they were daily notches.

The Indians had closed in on the twelfth day. The thirteenth day, "Laik wound." George Lake, his name misspelled. On the fourteenth day, "Bonn died." "Bonn" would have meant Bonniwell—Jim Bonniwell.

13

Lake wounded, Bonniwell dead. That eliminated Bonniwell and probably Lake who, if wounded in his hunger-weakened condition, must have died soon after.

Five names had been identified: George Lake, Jim Bonniwell, Douglas Carson, Axel Turnboom and Paul Slater. They had given him those names at the War Department, as they had been turned in by Fort Ogden, which in turn had listed the names from the evidence given in by Lieutenant Orpington. Letters, names on objects. Five bodies had been buried at Fort Starvation. It all checked.

But there had been six men at Fort Starvation.

The carvings on the logs . . . lies? Cut there later by the sixth man, to cover up. Lake? Bonniwell? Or . . . ?

A deadly whine smote Slater's eardrums. Outside the fort a horse uttered a wild, choked-off scream. The dull, yet sharp report of a rifle followed.

Slater whipped out his Navy Colt, reached the broken-down gate of the fort in four great leaps. His saddle horse was down, thrashing its legs in a death struggle, fifty yards from the fort. Off in the distance, a horseman galloped forward. Sun slashed on a rifle barrel.

The deadly whine came again; lead smacked into the earth three feet from where Slater stood and his ears were assailed again by the bark of a rifle.

He threw up his Navy gun, fired once, twice, a third time. The range was too far for a revolver, but the fact that he was in view and firing back caused the horseman to swerve aside, then wheel and go back another hundred yards. But then the rifle spoke a third time.

The range was about five hundred yards, a little far for accurate shooting from horseback, with a rifle. Too far for a revolver. The horseman, however, could dismount, throw himself prone to the ground and take better aim.

Slater whirled, leaped to his bed blanket of the night before and scooped up his rifle. He rushed back to the gate, dropped to the ground and took quick aim. The man in the distance must have guessed the reason for the sudden retreat and return, for he whirled his horse and galloped off. Slater fired once with his rifle, then gave it up.

He got to his feet and watched the would-be assassin disappear in the distance.

His saddle horse was dead. The pack horse was no good

for pursuit. He could leave his shovels and other equipment and ride the horse back to the Mormon settlement on the far side of the distant western mountain, but that was about all the animal was good for.

Slater turned and surveyed Fort Starvation once more. There was nothing more to be discovered, of that he was sure. The answer was not here.

4

To the west and north and south the White Sands rolled in undulating hills which moved as blew the wind; trackless, desolate waste that even the Indians avoided.

Slater had plodded across the white wasteland for two days and for one of those two days had carried a rifle and saddle. He had discarded them this morning or he would never have made the rutted trail that crawled along the eastern edge of the moving white sands.

He crouched now on his haunches and watched the stage-coach as it bore down upon him. As it neared, he got to his feet, but the stage driver seemed to have no intention of stopping for him. Not until Slater raised both hands, palms outward in the universal sign of peace.

The stage pulled to a creaking stop and fine sand swirled and enveloped Slater.

"Whaddya want?" cried the driver, dropping his hand to the butt of a revolver at his hip.

"A ride."

"How'd you get here?"

"My horse gave out yesterday morning."

The driver gestured to the White Sands. "Out there?"

A couple of faces showed along the side of the coach. The sun gleamed on metal in a man's hand. They were taking no chances. This was Apache country. Slater definitely was

16

not an Apache, but—well, there were white men out here worse than Apaches.

Slater said, "I can pay for the ride."

"Where to?" asked the driver.

"Tucson—if you go that far."

"I go there, all right," said the stage driver. "It's the end of the line." He sized up Slater a moment. "Got twenty dollars?"

Slater reached into a pocket and brought out some coins. He selected a twenty-dollar gold piece and tossed it up to the driver, who caught it.

"Climb aboard!"

Slater opened the door of the stage and climbed in. Before he had even seated himself, the whip cracked outside and the stage rolled away.

Besides Slater, there were three passengers in the stagecoach. A gray-whiskered man wearing a store suit of civilian clothes in which he had undoubtedly slept at least a hundred times; an Army officer, wearing the shoulder straps of a captain and the insignia of the Fourth Cavalry. The fourth passenger aboard the coach was the most beautiful woman Slater had ever seen. Slater looked at her covertly a second time and decided that she wasn't really a woman, but a girl of no more than twenty or twenty-one; a girl with golden hair, eyes as blue as the New Mexico sky on a cloudless day and finely chiseled features. She wore a velvet traveling dress of blue trimmed with mink or marten fur.

The Army officer spoke, "See any sign of the Apaches?"

Slater shrugged. "I came across the White Sands. . . .

The whiskered man exclaimed, "Even the Indians don't cross the White Sands."

"I was in a hurry," Slater said easily, then risked a third glance at the girl across from him. He met her eyes this time and quickly dropped his own.

"Lost your horse," the older traveler beside Slater was saying. "Heard you tell the driver. Must have been in a powerful hurry."

The cavalry captain shook his head. "Anyone's in a hurry traveling in this country." He scowled. "Sand and sagebrush, cactus and Apaches. If I had anything to say about it I'd give New Mexico and Arizona territories to the Indians and throw in half of Texas and Utah." He grunted. "By the way, my name's Beecham, Captain Leslie Beecham. And it's spelled that way, too, B-e-e-c-h-a-m, not B-e-a-u-c-h-a-m-p, or any other fancy way." Slater nodded recognition of the introduction, but did not volunteer his own name. The captain went on, however: "I wouldn't be out in this Godforsaken country if I didn't have to be. I go wherever they send me. Spent three years in Oregon——"

The girl spoke. "Did you like it better there, Captain?"

Her voice was rich, full, yet a little throaty. Slater's forehead creased a little. The voice tugged at his memory. As did her face. He was almost sure he had met her before. He had seen so few women in recent years he could almost count them on his fingers.

The captain had preferred Oregon, although he liked Minnesota even better than Oregon, except for the winters. Slater relaxed as much as he could in the jolting coach. He let his eyes become slits, close. The bouncing of the stage jarred them open. It was impossible to sleep, even to doze.

Then suddenly he opened his eyes wide. The girl across from him had mentioned Kansas. And now her eyes met Slater's again. Kansas—Lawrence, Kansas. But she couldn't be! Orpington's daughter had been a child in pigtails, a not too tidy girl, only half-grown. The one across from him now was mature, a beauty. It was only a few months . . .

She saw the recognition in his eyes and smiled. "Yes," she said.

He shook his head. "You've grown up!"

"I haven't grown a half inch."

A house dress, pigtails; living with a shiftless, drunken father.

"Say," exclaimed Captain Beecham, "you two know each other!"

"We've met," said Susan Orpington. To Slater, "Quite a ways from Kansas, isn't it?"

"Quite a ways," Slater conceded. He looked at Captain Beecham. "The colonel's gone back into the Army?"

Susan shook her head. "No, but he's been in Arizona Territory and when he heard that the captain was being assigned here . . ." She smiled, leaving the explanation unfinished.

Slater asked, "Colonel Orpington's in Tucson?"

"He's been there since right after you visited him. He's

going into business and he believes that Arizona is on the verge of a boom."

Lake was in Tucson, Sergeant Gilbert Lake, brother of George Lake, who had died at Fort Starvation.

The stage skirted the White Sands and stopped that night at the little town of Las Cruces, where the passengers spent the night in miserable rooms in a conglomeration of adobe buildings that was called a hotel.

Early the next morning, after a breakfast of tortillas and chili beans, the passengers again took their seats in the stage and were soon rolling westward. They slept that night at Lordsburg and the following day had a brush with Apaches, a scant half dozen who charged the stage, but beat a hasty retreat when the guns of the passengers opened up on them.

Two days later the stage rolled into Tucson, a cluster of adobe buildings, inhabited by Mexicans, fugitives from justice, Indians, Mexicans, a few soldiers, some businessmen and more Mexicans. Sheep, a few pigs, cats, a horde of dogs, burros and a few other specimens of the animal world roamed the streets.

The stage stopped before a two-story adobe building that bore the name Arizona House. Colonel Orpington was not at the hotel to greet his daughter, but a room had been reserved for her. Slater was assigned to one directly across the hall. He cleaned himself as well as he could with a small pitcher of water, then went down to the hotel lobby, which was merely a tiny anteroom for a thriving saloon that occupied most of the first floor. He caught the frowsy hotel clerk just coming out of the saloon, wiping his straggly mustache.

"How'll I get out to the fort?" Slater asked.

"You c'n ride out in the Army ambulance," was the reply, "on'y that's no good for you on account of you're a civilian and the Army ambulance is on'y for the Army." The clerk screwed up his lips. "Of course if you had some money you could rent a horse and ride out, but it ain't worth while since it's only a couple of miles. So I guess that leaves on'y walking."

"*If* I had the money to rent a horse, where would I get one?"

"At the livery stable; where else would you rent a horse?"

19

Slater turned away abruptly and walked out of the hotel. Almost directly across the street he saw the sign of a livery stable. Five minutes later he was astride a bay mare jogging out of Tucson toward the fort two miles away.

The fort was a sprawling, irregular mass of adobe buildings. Most of the buildings served as the walls of the fort and, where they did not touch, sections of wall had been built to connect them and made a continual wall around the enclosure of several acres.

Slater was a half mile from the fort when he heard pounding hoofs behind him. He half turned in his saddle. A buckboard was bearing down swiftly and he pulled his horse aside to let it pass. As it came up he saw that it was driven by Susan Orpington. He expected her to slow up for him, but she swirled past, barely nodding at him. Slater was thoughtful as he continued jogging toward the fort.

Discipline was lax. The sentry at the gate leaned against the adobe wall, looked at Slater and expectorated a half gill of tobacco juice. He did not challenge or question Slater.

Inside the fort, Slater tied his horse to a hitchrail and looked around for Headquarters. He saw a sign a short distance away and entered a narrow red adobe hut. Inside, a corporal with blouse unbuttoned slouched behind a scarred desk.

"I'm looking for Sergeant Gilbert Lake," Slater said.

The corporal shrugged. "So?"

"What's his troop?"

The corporal regarded him quizzically. "Lake's the toughest sergeant in the regiment. My money's on him—if you're looking for trouble."

"I'm not. I just want to talk to him."

"You don't mind waiting a little while, do you?"

"I've got plenty of time."

"All right, then wait around B Troop."

Slater nodded and started for the door. As he was about to go through, the corporal called after him, "About two weeks."

Slater turned. "What?"

"Lake'll be back in two weeks."

Slater gave the corporal a steady look and left the building. Outside, he stood under the wooden canopy and located the sign of Troop B across the parade ground.

20

He crossed and entered the orderly room. The first sergeant, a grizzled old soldier in his fifties, was working on the day book.

"I understand Sergeant Lake's in B Troop," Slater said.

The first sergeant looked up from his work. "Senior line sergeant. I can tell you that, but anything else you want to know about him, you'll have to ask the captain." He nodded toward a closed door at the rear of the orderly room.

Slater looked at the door, then back at the first sergeant. "I didn't say there was anything else I wanted to know about him."

"All right, I said Sergeant Lake was senior line sergeant of Troop B."

"I can see the captain?"

"When he gets through."

Slater looked through the windows at the buckboard standing outside the troop barracks. "Miss Orpington's with him?"

The first sergeant did not reply, for just then the door of the captain's office opened and she came out. She nodded coolly to Slater and brushed past him.

"Man to see you, sir," the first sergeant said to the captain of B Troop, a lean, dyspeptic-looking man of about forty.

"Come in," the captain said to Slater.

Slater crossed. "My name's John Slater."

"I'm Captain Welnick." The captain stood aside and let Slater enter his tiny office, then followed and closed the door.

The room was furnished with a small, scarred desk and two straight-backed chairs. The captain gestured for Slater to sit down.

Slater seated himself and said, "I really came to see Sergeant Lake, but I understand he's away from the fort at the moment."

"That's right." The captain seated himself behind his desk and looked inquiringly at Slater. "If it's important, I can send a message to him."

"It's personal." Slater regarded the captain thoughtfully. Would it be against regulations to tell me where the sergeant is?"

"It's not a military secret," Captain Welnick said coolly, "but we don't make it a rule to give out information about our men."

"I'm not asking you for information *about* Lake. I'm anxious to see him and I've come a long way. I thought if you could tell me where I might find him I'd go there to see him."

"He'll be back in a week, or ten days, at the most."

"I'd rather not wait that long."

"You're a relative?"

Slater shook his head. "My father knew his brother."

"His brother?" A flicker of interest showed in the captain's eyes. "His brother's dead."

"I know. He and my father died together . . . at Fort Starvation."

Captain Welnick grimaced. "Sergeant Lake's been with me a long time. Through the war and before. He—he told me what happened to his brother."

"Then you know that Miss Orpington's father was the one who found them?"

The captain exclaimed, "Why, no, I didn't . . ." His eyes went to the closed door, then he scowled and pushed his chair back a few inches. "Now see here, Slater!"

"Isn't that why she was here?" Slater asked crisply. "To talk to you about Lake?"

Captain Welnick got to his feet. "She never said a word about that. All right, it's none of your business, but I'll tell you, just so you don't go getting the wrong ideas. Colonel Orpington's an old friend of mine. We both commanded regiments in the same brigade during the war and I knew him at The Point—although he was three years ahead of me . . ." Welnick made an impatient gesture. "Orpington chose to resign from the Army. He's got to make a living and he's up at Cactus Springs right now where he's planning to buy a trading post. It's just outside the Chiricahua Reservation and it ought to be a good thing. That's why his daughter was here. She wants to join her father and since I'm sending a small detail there tomorrow, she asked if she could go along."

"Does Sergeant Lake happen to be anywhere near Cactus Springs?"

Captain Welnick's nostrils flared angrily. "He's in command of a detail I sent up to the reservation at the request of Hoffman, the Indian agent. Benton got scared." Welnick hesitated. "Hoffman's place is twenty miles from Cactus Springs —if that's what you wanted to know."

Slater got to his feet. "Thanks."

"Don't go getting any wrong ideas about Lake," Welnick growled. "He's been in the Army over twenty years. One of the best soldiers I've ever known."

"His kind are the backbone of the Army," Slater said.

Welnick regarded him suspiciously. "He's a man of little education and will remain a noncommissioned officer as long as he's in the Army. But he knows more about soldiering than most officers."

5

The detail consisted of a corporal and five privates. Two heavily laden pack mules trotted behind the last man, a line running from one to the other, then to the last private in the file.

The corporal rode in front and directly behind him was Susan Orpington. She wore buckskin riding skirt, a tan shirt and a short bolero style jacket.

Slater got up from under the meager shade of a tree and held up his hand. The corporal of the detachment, who had been watching Slater as he bore down on him, swung around the muzzle of his gun.

"You're going to run into trouble," Slater said. "There're smoke signals ahead."

"I seen them," retorted the corporal.

"You've heard the gunfire, too?"

The corporal squinted. "Who're you?"

Slater nodded to Susan Orpington. "Miss Orpington knows me."

The corporal shifted in his saddle so he could look back at Susan Orpington. She nodded. "Yes, I've met Captain Slater."

The corporal switched back to Slater. "Captain?"

"During the war." He inclined his head toward the rear. "The shooting's been intermittent, but fairly steady."

The corporal's forehead creased. "Benton's Store is that way, two—three miles . . ."

Susan Orpington spurred her horse forward. "Dad's at Benton's Store!"

Slater nodded. "I'm sorry, Miss Orpington. I thought you ought to know."

"It—it may not be . . ." She shot a sudden look at the corporal. "Please—let's hurry."

The corporal reached out and grabbed the bridle reins of Susan's horse. "Now, wait a minute, Miss. Captain Welnick gave me orders not to take any chances——"

"My father's up there. I—we've got to help him."

The corporal turned to Slater. "Now, see here, Mister, I haven't heard any shooting . . ."

"Listen!"

The corporal cocked his head sideward, held up his hand for the soldiers behind him to be silent. Gunfire came over distinctly; two shots, another, a pause, then three quick shots.

The corporal emitted a groan. "My orders was . . ." Then he exclaimed. "How many Indians would you say was up there, Captain?"

"That's hard to say. From the gunfire only four or five, but some of them may be, and probably are, armed with bows and arrows."

The corporal hesitated. You could see he was debating the matter and the decision was hard. Susan Orpington decided the matter. She spurred her horse forward, past the corporal. Slater smiled thinly, swung into the saddle of his own mount and sent it after Susan. Behind them the corporal roared, "Forward!"

There was no more gunfire. Not until the little cavalacade crested a rise and looked down upon the scene below, a flat stretch of ground, in the center of which stood a small cluster of adobe buildings. Behind a heap of rocks, some hundred yards from the trading post were eight or nine Indians, but there were twice that many horses.

Slater noted the disparity in the number of men and horses, gestured toward the trading post. "Hurry!"

From behind and to the right came a ragged volley of sudden gunfire. One of the soldiers cried out, tumbled from his saddle.

"Charge!" cried the corporal.

The little cavalacade swept down the hillside, onto the flat and toward the trading post. Behind them came a dozen yelling, shooting Apaches, half of them running afoot, the others mounted on wiry ponies. And down on the flat, the Apaches behind the rocks rose and poured their fire upon Slater's group.

The soldiers returned the fire vigorously, but caught between two groups of Indians, it would have been a losing proposition had not the defenders of the trading post suddenly spewed out of the doors and poured withering fire into the Indians by the rocks. The Indians dispersed and the relief detachment swirled down upon the trading post.

There was a quick flurry of greetings, then the entire party stormed into the trading post. Inside the men took positions by the windows. But there was a lull on the part of the Indians as they united and reorganized outside. That gave those inside the trading post time to get oriented.

Colonel Orpington came over to Slater. "We've met before."

"Your home in Lawrence a few months ago," Slater regarded the former Army officer speculatively. "Didn't expect to find you out here."

Susan Orpington said, "I met Captain Slater on the stagecoach. He's come here to find Sergeant Lake——"

A man wearing sergeant's chevrons perked up. "You mention my name?"

He was about forty-five and wore hash marks denoting twenty years of service; a professional soldier, an original hardcase. Slater had known a few oldtimers like him during the war. A fight was a day's work to them, no more.

Slater said, "How are you, Sergeant?"

Outside a gun banged and a slug crashed through an already shattered windowpane and thudded into the adobe wall beyond. A wild yell rose from the besieging Indians, and a dozen guns cracked and bullets whined and smashed into adobe and wood.

"Here they come!" shouted Benton, the trader.

Slater whirled to a broken window, thrust out his revolver and took a quick shot at an Indian on horseback. His bullet missed, for the Indian bobbed to the right and left, making a difficult target. Eighteen or twenty Indians were in the

26

charge, most of them armed with carbines of some sort, although a few had only bows and arrows. They bore down on the trading post, but before they reached it they fanned out and began circling the building. They yelled and screamed and fired their guns and discharged arrows from their bows.

Inside the trading post, the few defenders poured out a heavy fire, which, however, was more or less ineffective because of the tactics of the Apaches. A horse went down, but the rider bounced to the ground and went tearing back for the shelter of the rocks. Three guns were fired at him; the Indian went down, then came up again, reeling. But he reached the rocks and plunged down behind them.

6

The attack lasted less than a minute altogether, but it took its toll inside the trading post. Benton's skull was creased and a soldier suffered a severe wound in the arm.

The Indians drew off then, and the defenders took stock. Slater, for the first time, was able to size up the situation. Besides himself there was Benton, the trader, on the floor, moaning, the corporal and four privates, one of them wounded, Sergeant Lake and Colonel Orpington. And Susan Orpington. Also a supposedly friendly Apache who crouched in one corner of the trading post, Benton's man-of-all-work, who seemed to be taking no part in the defense of the place.

Orpington turned to Slater and Lake, his face grave. "We can't take any more attacks like that."

"We can stand as many as they can make," retorted Sergeant Lake. "We got plenty of grub and water." He grinned, gestured to a gun rack on the wall. "And guns!"

"What about tonight?" Slater asked.

"Apaches won't fight after dark."

"Maybe not, but they might try setting fire to the place."

"Ever try lightin' 'dobe? It don't burn. Like I said, we're in terrific shape." He paused, then grinned wryly. "Until tomorrow morning."

Slater frowned. "Why until tomorrow morning? You just said there was food, water and ammunition."

"Yep. We c'n lick this little bunch from now on—as long

as we're in here and they're out there. The only trouble is, they won't stay a small bunch like that."

"Reinforcements!" exclaimed Colonel Orpington.

"Right, sir. They c'n get them and they will—durin' the night. Us—" He called to the corporal who was bandaging the wounded trooper's arm. "Mizener, what were your orders?"

The corporal, on his knees beside the wounded man, turned. "We was to escort Miss Orpington here, that's all."

Sergeant Lake shrugged. "They'll expect you back the day after tomorrow. If you don't show up by the morning after they'll send out a detachment to look for you." He shook his head. "We won't be around that long. The 'Paches'll get help by tomorrow morning. That's all the time we've got."

Susan Orpington moved impulsively to her father's side, gripped his arm. "Dad, does that mean . . . ?"

"No!" exploded Colonel Orpington. "I'll be goddamned if it does. We're not going to get massacred by any piddling little bunch of savages. Not after"—he grimaced—"not after the things I've been through in my time."

Sergeant Lake shrugged and turned up the palms of both hands expressively. "Don't sound right, does it, Colonel? Me, I seen a little action myself here and there. Never thought I'd wind up like this. Although I don't see what difference it makes. One of those little black boys c'n kill you just as dead as anyone else."

"There must be a way out of this," stormed Orpington. He turned, saw the wounded Benton sitting up. "Benton, you've lived around these people—you ought to know them as well as anyone."

"I do," groaned Benton. He dabbed at his creased skull, brought the hand away covered with gore, and groaned louder. "Kill every damn one of them, that's what they ought to do. They're animals, that's all. They ain't human. . . ."

"Maybe some of our people haven't treated them exactly human," Slater said pointedly.

"You can't treat them human," persisted Benton. "They're savages. I say kill 'em all."

"Go right ahead, Mister," said Sergeant Lake. "An' while you're killing 'em, we'll figure out a way to get out of this." He looked at Orpington. "Mind if I make a suggestion?"

Orpington made an impatient gesture. "I'm not in the Army any more. We're all in this together equally."

Sergeant Lake nodded sagely. "Well, sir, here's the way I see it. We can't just sit here and hope to stand off the Indians until relief comes, because tomorrow morning those eighteen-twenty Indians out there may be fifty or a hundred. We can't fight that many. That means we've got to get out of here before morning."

"How?" Slater asked bluntly.

"That's the problem."

Colonel Orpington, who had been listening intently to the sergeant, began to scowl. "You've got a solution to that problem?"

"No, but since we know what the problem is we can concentrate on it."

A carbine cracked outside and a bullet zinged through a broken window and plunked into the wall. Sergeant Lake left the group, stepped to the window and, thrusting out his revolver, fired two quick shots.

"Just to let 'em know we're watching," he said laconically, and returned to Orpington and Slater. "What I was going to say was, we ain't outnumbered so much, two-three to one. We can make a break for it and some of us may get through."

"On foot?" cried Benton. "They'll run us down in no time. We ain't got a chance."

Sergeant Lake regarded Benton steadily. "On the other hand, we c'n try to make a deal with the 'Paches. They ain't really mad at but one of us and if we give 'em that fella, they might——"

"No!" screamed Benton. "You wouldn't do that—you wouldn't!"

"Then shut your trap awhile," Lake said calmly.

Benton appealed wildly to Colonel Orpington. "You wouldn't let him do that, Colonel. It wouldn't be human." He gripped Orpington's coat lapel eagerly. "You offered three thousand for the tradin' post. I—I'll sell it cheap. T-two thousand. Fifteen hundred, if you get me out of here. That—that's a real bargain. Fifteen hun'erd——"

Orpington shoved the craven trader away from him. "Don't be a bigger fool than you have to be, Benton. What you've got to sell right now isn't worth a Confederate shinplaster."

"A—a thousand d-dollars . . ."

Orpington turned his back on the man. "We haven't any choice in the matter, Sergeant. Your plan is the only one." His eyes went to Susan.

Lake made note of it and shrugged. "Oh, we'll cover her, of course."

"You'll do nothing of the kind," Susan Orpington declared. "I'll take my chances with everyone else. Besides how long would I last in this country . . . alone?"

"It'll be night, Susan," her father said gruffly. "You can get quite a ways from here before morning."

"She can get farther with a horse," Slater suggested. "And so can all of us."

"On'y horses is somethin' we ain't got," Sergeant Lake pointed out.

Slater stepped to the window, peered out, then signaled to Lake and Orpington. "Look."

The two men stepped to the window. Lake exclaimed immediately. "They moved them."

"Naturally. We could pick them off from here." Slater paused a moment. "One or two of us can head for the horses, drive off those we don't want, so the Indians can't use them to follow us and bring the rest down here—close enough so the others have a chance to get to them."

Colonel Orpington pursed up his lips and nodded slowly. "That's it. Yes, that's the thing to do. Two men go after the horses. We'll wait here for the signal, then when it comes, make a rush. The element of surprise."

And then Slater noted that the Apache man-of-all-work was no longer crouched in the corner. He sent a quick searching look around the room, then pointed at Benton.

"The Indian—where is he?"

Benton looked stupidly at Slater. "Somewhere around."

Sergeant Lake was already dashing for the door, which led to a storeroom in the rear. He went in, came out immediately.

"Window's open. He's gone!"

Colonel Orpington let out a roar. "You blithering idiot," he yelled at Benton. "You said yourself they were all murdering savages and now you've let him go out and tell his friends our plan."

"I wasn't watchin' him," whined Benton. "Didn't figure

there was any call to. He—he's worked for me two-three years."

Sergeant Lake signaled to one of the soldiers. "Get into the back room. Nail some boards across the window. We've got enough to watch out here."

The soldier trotted into the back room. In a moment he started hammering.

Lake, Orpington and Slater gathered together again. Lake shook his head. "Guess I shoulda kept an eye on him."

"He may not have heard the whole plan," Slater said. "In fact, I'm quite sure he didn't hear about the horses. My mind wasn't on him, but I seem to remember shooting a look around before I suggested the horse plan."

"If he heard it, we're dead," said Orpington morosely. Then he drew a deep breath and exhaled heavily. "It's still the only thing we can do. Two men to go for the horses." He cleared his throat. "And I don't feel we can order any of the men to do it. It'll have to be volunteers."

Sergeant Lake looked inquiringly at Slater. The latter nodded.

"Me and Cap'n Slater," Lake said.

Colonel Orpington exclaimed, "We can draw straws for it. Just because I was once an officer . . ."

"S'all right," said Lake. "We volunteered."

Orpington hesitated, then nodded brusquely. "Good. There's an early moon tonight, so the sooner we make the break after dark, the better."

"Good enough," said Slater. "We've got a couple of hours. I suggest we all get something to eat. What've you got, Benton?"

"I dunno," replied the trader. "Victoriano's squaw did the cookin'. Ain't seen her around all day."

"You've got some canned goods on the shelves," Slater suggested.

"Yeah, sure." Benton shrugged. "Might as well eat it up. When those Injuns get in here they won't leave a thing, anyway." He shot a quick look at Colonel Orpington, moistened his tongue, then thought better of what he had been about to say, and moved to the store shelves.

Sergeant Lake, meanwhile, got into a low discussion with the corporal, which resulted in the latter's going to the gun rack and examining the guns. Slater stepped to one of the windows and, peering out, studied the layout of the Apaches' defense.

They were behind the rocks now, but when nightfall came he knew some of them would disperse and take up strategic spots where they could watch the trading post from all sides. He and Lake would not find it easy to get past the sentries.

The Indian horses were nowhere in sight, but Lake guessed that they would be over the ridge in the direction from which they had approached the trading post a half hour ago. It was the closest real shelter, a half mile from the post, perhaps, and not too far from where the Indians were at the moment.

It would still be a difficult job for two men. Slater thought the chances were in the Indians' favor.

7

He turned from the window to see Colonel Orpington talking earnestly to his daughter. Sergeant Lake, out of range of the windows, was leaning against the store counter watching him. He smiled as his eyes met Slater's.

"Think we'll make it?"

"As you said yourself—we can be killed just as dead in here as out there."

The sergeant chuckled. "That's the way I look at it. Inside, or outside, gun, arrow, it don't make any difference. If you're going to get it, you're going to get it."

Slater crossed to the sergeant. "Your brother and my father were in a spot very like this."

Lake's eyes became slits. "Slater, eh?" He could not resist shooting a look at Colonel Orpington across the room and Slater knew that the colonel had already talked to him on this topic. Lake nodded slowly. "First him, then you. What's it all about?"

Both Orpington and Susan came over. They had apparently heard the trend of the conversation between Lake and Slater. "Mr. Slater," Orpington said bluntly. "My daughter's just told me the reason for your being here."

"Same as yours, isn't it?"

"How do you figure? I came to Arizona to go into business."

"And you just happened to pick a section of Arizona where Sergeant Lake happened to be."

The colonel's eyes glowed and Slater saw that he was making an effort to control his temper. Susan Orpington stepped into the breach.

"Dad—please. He didn't mean that the way it sounds."

"I meant," Slater said deliberately, "that Colonel Orpington came to Arizona for the same reason I did—to pump Sergeant Lake."

"Hey, wait a minute, folks!" exclaimed Sergeant Lake. "I don't understand all this. Why should you people be interested in *me?*"

"Father was the officer in charge of the soldiers who found Fort Starvation," Susan said quickly. "Back in 1861."

Lake's face showed astonishment; Slater was almost inclined to believe that it was genuine.

Lake said, "That was my older brother—not me."

"We know that," Susan Orpington continued smoothly. "The fact of the matter is, Mr. Slater suspects my father. He believes that he is after some gold that your brother and—and the others—were supposed to have hidden near this fort!"

"News to me," said Lake. Then he cocked his head to one side. "I wonder . . ."

Slater's lean face went forward to watch the sergeant more closely. Orpington caught it, too. "Your brother wrote you, Sergeant!"

"Once every year or two. And I saw him about that often. Last time was, let me see, 1858 or maybe it was '57. Yeah, come to think of it, I was stationed in Oregon Territory when he dropped in on me, out of a clear sky. He'd been down in California." He paused. "Prospecting." He looked thoughtfully at Orpington. "He struck it rich, you say?"

"*I* didn't say so," snapped Colonel Orpington.

A bullet came through the window and two of the soldiers returned the fire and added a few shots for interest. The group by the counter waited until the exchange of shots was finished, then Slater took the initiative.

"I'm not looking for gold, Sergeant."

"That's what you say," blustered Orpington. "Sixty thousand—is——"

"A helluva lot of money," finished Slater, then apologized. "Excuse me, Miss Orpington."

"It's all right. As you were saying, sixty thousand is a hell of a lot of money."

She repeated the salty figure of speech so matter of factly that Slater looked at her with sudden interest. An Army brat, she had probably got used to swearing by the time she was ten years old.

He said, "Colonel Orpington's detachment buried five men. I happen to know there were six at Fort Starvation."

Lake seemed puzzled. "Five or six, what's the difference? They were all killed."

"That's the point, Sergeant. *Were* they all killed?"

Lake hesitated a moment. "I see what you mean. Yeah, I got the report from the Army, back in '61. Not very nice. Some of them, uh, weren't killed. They—well, they starved to death."

"You're still not getting the point," Slater persisted. "The remains of *five* men were buried. But there were *six* men at the fort. That's what I'm trying to determine. What happened to the sixth man?"

"You think he got away?"

"No, no," interrupted Orpington. "Mr. Slater's much more, shall we say—insidious—than that. He thinks this sixth man may have betrayed the others to the Indians."

"What difference does that make today? All this happened years ago. They're dead and it don't make . . ." Then Lake paused. For the first time Slater saw the sergeant's face become a mask.

"Don't you see, Sergeant?" he asked evenly. "It makes quite a difference. Think of how they died——"

"And think of the sixty thousand in gold," Susan Orpington said, and whirled away from the group.

Lake watched her cross to one side of the room. Then he looked at both Orpington and Slater and shook his head.

"Let me think this over a minute."

He walked in the opposite direction from Susan, went to a keg and sat down on it.

Behind the counter, Benton slammed tin cans around. "Food's ready," he snapped. "Come and get it."

Slater signaled to the soldiers by the windows. As they left their posts to eat, he moved to the window to stand guard. Orpington scowled mightily, looked at Slater, at Lake, then moved to Susan's side. He began talking to her in a hoarse whisper, but Susan shook her head in annoyance and he subsided.

Lake did not eat. The soldiers ate as much as they wanted, then Slater ate a can of corned beef and a couple of pieces of biscuit. Susan ate a meager mouthful and then Orpington finished what was left.

All the while Lake remained seated on the keg, wrapped in heavy, and from the look on his face not pleasant, thought. Slater let him alone. After a while he went to the gun rack and took down a pair of Colt revolvers. Benton watched him load them. Then he said, "Those guns're worth twenty dollars apiece."

"I'll pay you for them tomorrow," Slater retorted. He thrust the two guns down the waistband of his trousers.

Darkness came slowly. The Indians kept up an intermittent fire, which was returned by the defenders of the trading post. With nightfall the shooting outside lessened. But some of the soldiers, watching closely, fired at fleeting shadows which were the Indians deploying to surround the place. It was not known whether the soldiers scored any hits.

When it was almost too dark to see one another inside the trading post, Orpington came to Slater. "About time, isn't it?"

"I'm ready whenever the sergeant is."

Orpington turned toward Lake. "How about it, Sergeant?"

Lake got slowly to his feet. "I guess so." He came over to Slater and Orpington. "You think my brother's alive?" he asked, addressing Slater.

"I didn't say that. I said one of the men who was at Fort Starvation was not buried there."

"We buried everyone who was there," Orpington said doggedly.

"Yes, I'm sure you did," replied Slater. "But one of the men walked away—alive. I want to find that man."

"Who could be my brother?" Lake asked.

"You've had time to think it over." Slater paused. *"Is it your brother?"*

It was too dark to see Lake's face, but there was a pause before he replied, "I don't know."

Slater seized upon that. "Don't you know?" He caught

Lake's arm in the gloom. "You're not sure he's dead? Why? What makes you think he might be alive?"

"I told you I don't know," snapped Lake angrily. He jerked his muscular arm clear of Slater's hard grip. "When there's sixty thousand dollars involved, a man doesn't know much of anything."

Now Orpington began to prod Lake. "You're going out there in a few minutes. You know what the risk is. If there's anything you've got to say now's the time."

"I haven't got anything to say." Then Lake suddenly snarled. "*You're* going out there, too. Your chance of pulling through is as thin as mine." He gestured to Slater. "Come on, Captain, it's dark enough."

"I'm just going to say one thing more," Slater said remorselessly. "My father's dead——"

"How do *I* know that?"

"I'm telling you."

"That isn't good enough. Not when there's sixty thousand dollars concerned."

"All right, Sergeant," Slater said hopelessly. "Let's go."

Lake slammed away from Slater, went around the counter and got himself a second revolver. He loaded it, then headed for the door to the shed in the rear.

Slater started to follow and a small, cool hand reached out of the darkness and found his own. There was a quick pressure, then the hand was removed.

"Good luck," Susan Orpington said softly.

Slater groped his way to the storeroom in the rear, where Lake was talking to one of the soldiers. "We're going through the door. The minute we're out, put up the bar and go back into the other room."

"All right, Sergeant."

"And don't try to be a hero," Lake warned. "If you hear shooting, stay where you are. We're taking our chances, same as the rest of you. Don't come out, no matter what you hear. Until we're out front with the horses. Ready, Captain?"

"Ready."

The soldiers removed the bar from the rear door and stepped back with it. Lake gripped the doorknob, turned it and pulled the door open wide enough for a man to slip

38

through. Slater, touching him, felt Lake pass through the door. He drew a deep breath and followed.

"Down!" came Lake's quick whisper.

Slater dropped to the ground. Lake's hand touched his elbow. "I think we ought to go straight ahead until we get clear, then circle around to the hills."

"You know more about this sort of thing than I do," Slater replied. "Lead the way."

8

Lake came up to his hands and knees, scurried along sound-lessly for three or four yards, then dropped flat to his stom-ach. Slater followed as best he could, but knew that he wasn't being as quiet as Lake and the latter cautioned him about it.

"You can't make that much noise," he said in a low whis-per. "These 'Paches have good ears. They can hear a rattle-snake at fifty yards."

"All right, I'll try."

Lake, however, adopted a new mode of traveling. He began worming over the ground, using his hands and elbows to pull himself along. Slater imitated him as closely as he could and thought that he made less noise. Their progress, however, was much slower. They covered perhaps fifty yards in the first ten minutes, but then Lake decreased the pace even more and the next fifty yards took them a good half hour. Slater became impatient.

"Can't we travel faster?" he asked in a low whisper.

Lake's hand snaked out and gripped Slater's arm.

Slater thought Lake's grip merely a caution to keep quiet, but Lake retained the grip and remained motionless. Slater, peering ahead for a long moment, then made out a small mound ahead and slightly to the left. After a moment's watching he thought the mound moved slightly. A little shiver ran through him. An Indian, hunkered down on his heels.

Had he heard Slater's whisper? If he had, the Indian had

not located them, and was keeping motionless himself, hoping to blend with the shadows.

Lake's grip slowly relaxed on Slater's arm, then the hand was removed. Slater continued to remain motionless, then became aware suddenly that Lake was no longer at his side. He had moved forward soundlessly.

Slater started to follow, then stopped. Lake was moving toward the Indian, his purpose obvious. Slater, if he made a noise, would put Lake in jeopardy. He strained his eyes to follow the slow movement of the shadow that was Lake, as it closed the gap between him and the Indian ahead.

Two minutes, three. Then Lake's shadow rose suddenly. There was a crunch of a boot on hard earth, a startled exclamation, cut off by a heavy thud as Lake's gun smashed in the Apache's skull.

Lake called then, in a hoarse whisper, "All right, Slater!"

Slater, assuming there would not be another Indian too near, scurried over the ground to Lake's side.

"He's a good Indian," Lake whispered. "Now, straight ahead some more."

Again the two men began their forward movement, but this time Lake led a faster pace and after ten minutes, came up to his knees.

"I think we're clear," he said, and got to his feet.

"The moon's coming up."

"I know. If we'd started later we couldn't have made it."

They were a good half mile from the trading post, but went ahead another half mile, walking swiftly, before they began to circle to the south. The moon was up well now and they could make out the hills without any trouble. And far to their left, they could see a huddle of shadows that was the trading post.

They walked perhaps three miles before they hit the rutted trail that led from the hills to the trading post. They crossed the trail some fifty yards or so, then turned due south. Lake cautioned Slater again.

"There'll be a guard with the horses."

Walking stooped, the two men climbed a rough ridge. As they reached the crest of it, Lake dropped to his knees. Slater heard the horses first, but for a moment or two he could not locate them. Lake pointed to a clump of cottonwood trees some hundred yards from where they crouched.

"Picket line," he said.

"We need eight horses altogether. Ride one, lead three."

They moved cautiously down the slope, reached the edge of the cottonwoods and could then see the horses inside a small glade, separated from them by a fringe of trees.

"Where's the guard?" whispered Slater.

"I don't know. Probably on the ground, where it's too dark to locate him. We'll have to make him show himself."

Lake drew his gun and got to his feet. Slater followed the example. Crouched low the two men moved toward the trees. Then a streak of fire lanced toward them. Lake cried out and fired his gun once, twice. Slater rushed forward and stumbled across the fallen Indian. He turned.

"You got him! Are you hit?"

"No. But we've got to work fast now."

Lake came swiftly forward and Slater followed him to the picket line, where some twenty or more horses were tied. The animals were skittish, but Lake moved among them with a sureness engendered from twenty years in the cavalry. He cut a long length of the picket rope, ran it through the rope halters of three of the Indian ponies and handed the end of the rope to Slater.

Slater mounted a fourth horse, then waited for Lake to rope up three more horses, which took him only seconds so fast did the cavalryman work. Lake swung up on a horse.

"Let's go!" he cried.

He drew a revolver and fired it into the air. Slater emptied one of his own guns and there was a wild stampede as the Indian ponies dispersed.

Slater had difficulty with his own horses, who were inclined to stampede but he kept a firm grip on the lead rope and followed Lake out of the cottonwoods. Lake put his pony into a gallop and Slater followed him. They were riding bareback, of course, but Slater kept his knees pressed tightly into the belly of his mount and urged it forward continuously.

They crested the ridge and headed down the incline toward the trading post at full speed.

Although the drumming of their horses' hoofs drowned out the sound of gunfire, the flashes of fire from the trading post—and from outside—told them that an exchange of gunfire was going on.

42

And then bullets began zinging through the air, at Lake and Slater. Darts of flame shot at them from different directions. Slater bent low over his pony's head.

The gunfire ahead became audible as they neared the trading post. The pin points of fire came closer to the buildings, as the Indians rushed to get between the horses and the post.

They were a hundred yards from the trading post when the besieged came through the door. Guns banged furiously and a dozen streaks of fire lanced from just outside the door of the main building. Lake's horses swirled down and Slater was just behind him.

For a moment there was tremendous confusion as the horses milled, as people mounted and fought Apaches who charged forward. Slater suffered a numbing blow on his right arm, which caused him to drop the gun he had in his hand. The picket rope was torn from his other hand.

Yells of Indians as well as soldiers punctuated the pounding of the horses' hoofs and the gunfire. Then, suddenly, Slater was galloping away from the trading post, and there was galloping all around him. There was more gunfire and more yelling, but in the yelling there was a note of rage and frustration.

A figure on the ground appeared before Slater. Flame lanced at him and he felt a tug at his collar. Then his horse struck something and stumbled. Slater was almost unseated, but when he recovered his balance all was clear before him.

The horses had scattered. One was running ahead of him and another was pounding directly behind him, but the rest were fanning out, each headed in a different direction.

Slater caught glimpses of rocks and trees as he raced along and knew that he was in the rough country south of the trading post. He did not slacken the speed of his horse, however, even when the animal began to pant and heave.

He kept his eyes on the horse ahead of him, swerved his own to follow as the lead horse turned. The hoofs behind him died out and he realized after a while that he and the rider ahead were alone.

His mount was in great distress and Slater considered pulling it up when he became suddenly aware that the animal ahead of him was riderless. He pulled up his own horse so violently that it stumbled and threw him. He hit the dirt heavily and when he gained his feet, the horse that had carried him until now was lost in the gloom of the hills.

A low groan came from the right. Slater whipped out his remaining revolver and cocked it.

"Who is it?"

"You, Slater?" asked the weak voice of Sergeant Lake.

Slater moved swiftly forward dropped to his knees beside the other man. He gripped the man, started to raise him to a sitting position, then realized that his hand was wet. He lowered Lake again.

"You're hit!"

"Indian got me . . . when we got the horses . . ."

Slater exclaimed, "You said he missed you."

"We had to—had to get the horses to the post." Lake coughed wrackingly. "How many got away?"

"I don't know. Most of them, I guess. Take it easy, now, while I see how badly you're hurt."

"No use. Held on as long as I could. Be gone . . . in a little while."

Slater brushed aside the soldier's feeble protests, opened his shirt. He felt gently of the wounded man's chest and when he found the wound, wondered what had kept him alive until now. It was a huge gaping hole almost in the center of the chest, perhaps an inch to the left. He took a handkerchief from his pocket and placed it gently over the wound.

"Bad?" asked Lake.

Slater hesitated, then decided that the sergeant had the right to know. "I'm afraid so."

"How—how long?"

"I don't know."

"You were in the war. You've seen wounds. I—I'd like to know."

"All right," Slater said harshly. "Minutes."

Lake took it well. He was silent for a long minute and Slater thought he was praying, but then the dying man spoke. "It don't seem to make much difference now. Sixty thousand. . . . Orpington . . . Orpington wants that money."

"All he knows is the Army and he couldn't stand it any more because he didn't go up in rank like his friends. He resigned and he's broke now."

44

"You, Slater," Lake said with effort, "I can't make you out. It—it *isn't* the money with you."

"They told you how my father—and your brother—died." Slater paused. "*If* your brother died."

Lake groaned. "I tell you, I don't know. I—I was sure, but two—no, three years ago, a man came around . . ."

Slater bent lower. "Who was he?"

"The name he used wasn't his real one. All right, Johnston, that's what he called himself. Al Johnston. Said he was one of the soldiers who buried my brother——"

"One of Orpington's men?"

"He didn't mention Orpington's name. The name Al Johnston—that didn't go with me at all. Albert Sidney Johnston was in command of the troops in Utah at the time. He—he died at Shiloh. But you know that."

"Of course. If he hadn't died you'd have never heard of Lee. Johnston was the best. But—this man, what did he want?"

"Information. About—about my brother. Asked if I had any of his letters . . ."

"Did you?"

"I'm an enlisted man. How much stuff can I accumulate? Never kept any letters. He—he hinted that maybe my brother wasn't dead. Said I might be able to find him if—if I remembered everything he'd written in the letters . . ."

Lake's speech was becoming labored. He stopped for a moment, closing his eyes, then resumed haltingly.

"He was no good. Knew it. Shifty. On—on the dodge——"

"Who? Your brother?"

"No. John—Johnston. Hung around. Took—took shot at me once. Then skipped. Horse had a Texas brand. Looked it up. No—no good . . ."

A low groan was forced from Lake's lips. His body quivered as his lungs sucked in air. He was at the end of the trail. Slater looked moodily down at him. It wasn't a good death, out here with the Apaches all around. Slater wouldn't even be able to bury him.

Yet—would Slater's own end be much different? An Apache bullet might strike him down at any moment. And if not an Apache . . . ?

Words came again from Lake's mouth. Words Slater had no right to hear. Things about Lake's childhood, his mother, a sister who had died in childhood. Then . . . George.

"Don't, George. Don't—do it!" Lake's voice rose in sudden frenzy. "Don't, George!"

Something from their childhood? Slater put his hand on Lake's shoulder, shook him gently. Lake's voice trailed off and he began moaning. Another minute . . .

"Lake!" Slater said sharply. Then in the voice of command: *"Sergeant Lake!"*

"Y-yes, sir!" The reply was torn from Lake.

"This man who came to you, Al Johnston, you said he was on the dodge. How did you *know he was on the dodge?"*

Lake's eyes opened wide, seemed to bulge. *"Gave me gold piece. Denver mint. . . . Clark and Gruber. . . . Stolen— stolen in hold . . ."*

Blood gushed from Lake's mouth, stopped and he was dead. Slater remained kneeling beside him for a long moment, then got slowly to his feet.

He looked around. The ponies he and Lake had ridden were nowhere in sight. He shook his head, began walking into the night.

9

Captain Welnick of Troop B sprang to his feet as Slater entered the captain's office. "Lord, man, we thought you were——"

"Someone's come through?"

"Yesterday. Colonel Orpington, his daughter, Benton the trader and—and Private Weisinger." He moved aside a step to look past Slater, to see if anyone was out in the other room. "Sergeant Lake?"

Slater shook his head. "I'm sorry."

"I was afraid he was done for. Those Apaches will get a lesson they won't forget for a long time. Two companies are out already, and Troops B and L go out in the morning."

"All because a trader cheated the Indians."

Captain Welnick grimaced. "I know. Benton. We've had complaints about him before. But that's not for me to say. Or the commander of this post. Indian policy is determined in Washington."

"You got a report from Colonel Orpington?"

The captain nodded. "Yes, he told how Sergeant Lake went through the lines and brought up the horses."

"Lake, alone?"

Captain Welnick cocked his head to one side. "What do you mean—it wasn't Lake who got the horses?"

"Oh yes, it was Lake, all right. I thought Orpington might have added something to the report." Slater made an impatient gesture. "It doesn't matter. I just wanted to tell you about Lake. I was with him when he died. He was shot when he got the horses. He *could* have climbed on a horse and cleared out and nobody would have blamed him, and nobody would have known just what had happened down at the trading post. But he didn't do that. Wounded, he took the horses through the Apaches, to the trading post, helped to fight off the Indians, then finally made his own getaway . . . and died as a result of it. I thought," Slater added heavily, "that you might want to put that in your report."

"I will, and thank you." Welnick cleared his throat. "About Orpington's report." He hesitated. "Well, about Colonel Orpington. You understand, Captain, you were a volunteer officer during the war. You, ah, well, what I mean to say is, you were not West Point."

"I understand perfectly, Captain. West Pointers stick together . . . against the rest of the world."

Captain Welnick frowned. "I wouldn't say just that. Only West Point is a school like any other school. It's only natural that men who went to the same school have something special in common.

"Certainly. A West Pointer was selling wood on the streets of St. Louis ten years ago. It was only natural that West Pointers should go out of their way to buy wood from him."

Captain Welnick's face got quite red. "The history of General Grant is well known. . . . You're not an easy man to talk to, Mr. Slater."

"I just came in to tell you about Sergeant Lake. An enlisted man, Captain, not an officer."

Slater turned and walked out of Captain Welnick's office. As he left the barracks of Troop M, he was hailed by Benton, the trader, who was hurrying toward him.

"Slater! Just a minute."

Slater stopped and the trader came up. There was a dirty bandage about his head, but otherwise he showed no ill effects from the battle at his trading post.

"They're goin' to wipe out those damn 'Paches," the trader exulted. "Teach 'em to go murderin' white folks."

"I just remembered," Slater said. "I said I'd pay you for that revolver of yours I took at the store."

Benton's face brightened. "That's right."

"All right," said Slater. "Here's your pay . . ." He suddenly smashed the trader a savage blow in the face. Benton cried out and hit the ground heavily. By the time he struggled to his feet, Slater had gone on.

In Tucson, Slater got a room at the hotel, cleaned himself, then returned to the desk.

"What room has Colonel Orpington got?" he asked the clerk.

The man shook his head. "Checked out."

"And Miss Orpington?"

"Went with him. They took the east stage this morning." The clerk grunted. "Had enough of Arizona. Can't say's I blame them. Almost got killed by 'Paches up north of here. Had a helluva fight and only got through by the skin of their teeth."

A city they called Denver was now sprawled up and down the mountainside where rattlesnakes and prairie dogs had sunned themselves twelve years ago. They were even talking about building a railroad north to meet the Union Pacific, and a man named Palmer was going around with some wild talk about building a railroad south from Denver to the Rio Grande.

Denver boasted a government mint, where they made gold and silver coins from native Colorado metal. The squat, heavyset man, Allison, who was in charge of the mint, pushed the two twenty-dollar gold pieces toward Slater.

"Feel 'em."

Slater picked up the double eagles one at a time, felt them and clinked them on the counter, one after the other. Then he picked up one of them again.

"This one's got a duller ring."

Allison bobbed his head. "Solid gold. Twenty dollars' worth of gold in it—well, not quite, 'cause some of it's worn off. But that was the trouble with those pure gold coins. They were too soft and wore down too quickly. The other one's got an alloy in it—makes the coin harder, but there's only about nineteen dollars and fifty cents' worth in it." He chuckled. "People around here still prefer the Gruber double eagles, when they can get them. We buy them up whenever we can, melt them down and make new coins from them. Cheaper coins. Of course, there are still a lot of the coins outstanding, but we don't care too much about the quarter

49

eagle, half eagle and eagles. Even Clark and Gruber put alloy into those after the first few months. It's only the double eagle they kept pure. They never used an alloy in those, except for that last small batch."

"What batch was that?"

"Right before we took over. You understand that when the government decided to establish a mint here, there was no longer any reason for Clark and Gruber—or the other private mints—to make currency. Fact is, Clark and Gruber sold the government their equipment. We're using it right now."

"About those alloyed twenty-dollar pieces," Slater persisted, "that last batch Clark and Gruber struck off—"

The dawn of suspicion began to show in Allison's eyes. "What about them?"

"I don't know. I'm asking you."

Allison took several seconds to think of his reply. Then he said, "Only five hundred of those were coined—ten thousand dollars." He paused again. "Have you ever seen any of them?"

"Yes." Slater touched one of the gold pieces before him. "That's one, isn't it?"

The mint man nodded. "It's one of three that have come back."

"What happened to the others? Worn out?"

"Uh-uh. No. At least, I don't think so." Allison pursed up his lips. "You're sure you don't know?"

"Quite sure."

"Then how come you asked?"

It was Slater's turn to hesitate. Then he took a chance. "Those three coins you say came back here, did a man named Lake have anything to do with one of them?"

"Perhaps. Why?"

"Because a sergeant in the Fourth Cavalry died about a week ago. He started to tell me about a Gruber double eagle, but died before he could get out much."

Allison drew a deep breath. "All right, if you don't know, you can find out easily enough from the newspapers. The five hundred Clark and Gruber double eagles, like this one, were shipped from the mint by stagecoach to Cripple Creek in the early fall of '61. They never got there. The mint immediately issued a statement that the coins could be identified and as a result none ever appeared in circulation . . . not until three years ago, when three of them dribbled in here. We were able to trace back only one, to a Sergeant Gilbert Lake of the Fourth Cavalry. He claimed it had been given to him by a stranger. Only Sergeant Lake's long record in the Fourth Cavalry got him out of that."

"Thanks," said Slater. "As you said, I could have gotten that from the newspapers, but you saved me the trouble, so thanks."

He nodded, started to turn away. Allison said quickly, "You say your name is Slater?"

"That's right. And I'm staying at the Black Hotel. I'll be there until tomorrow, at least . . . if you're planning to send over the sheriff."

"Oh, not the sheriff!"

10

Slater left the mint and walked up the street to the Black Hotel, one of the better ones of the eight or ten hotels that the city of Denver already boasted.

He got his key at the desk and climbed the stairs to the second floor. He put the key in the lock, but couldn't turn it, for the door was already unlocked. Slater touched his right hand to his left coat lapel for a quick draw from his shoulder holster, and pushed open the door with his left hand.

Susan Orpington was seated in a chair, facing the door. She smiled at him lazily.

"Hello, Captain."

Slater closed the door and removed his right hand from his coat lapel. "Hello," he said.

"How are things at the mint?" Susan Orpington asked.

"They're doing an excellent business in dimes and quarters," Slater replied drily. "Not so good in dollars, however. If that's what you wanted to talk about."

"It isn't. Dad was in such a hurry to leave Arizona that I didn't get a chance to say good-bye to you. Or thank you for helping us out. I understand Sergeant Lake didn't make it."

"No, he didn't. The colonel's with you?"

"Not here—no. I thought I could get farther without him. For some reason you and he don't get along very well."

She got up from the chair and, crossing to a table, turned to face him as she leaned back lightly against the table.

"You've grown quite a lot since I saw you in Lawrence," Slater said.

"Just how old do you think I am?"

"About eighteen. Although when I saw you in Lawrence I would have guessed about fourteen."

"I happen to be twenty."

"Your father's planning to buy a business in Denver?"

She smiled indulgently. "At least we can drop *that* fiction. Dad's no businessman. He's tried it several times."

"Since the war?"

"Since, and before."

"Before the war? I thought he was in the Army."

"He was. But there's no law against officers engaging in business on the side. The Army recognizes that the pay of a— a first lieutenant isn't enough to support a family. They don't mind if an officer engages in a business venture, as long as it doesn't interfere with his Army duties. When I was five, Dad had a grocery store in California. Grocers got rich in those days—but not Dad. In North Carolina he bought a half interest in a tannery, just before it went into bankruptcy."

"Then why doesn't he go back into the Army?"

"As a captain? At his age? He wouldn't like that. And neither would I. And it won't be necessary. With the forty thousand dollars we can make out quite well."

"Forty thousand? The amount is sixty."

"The full amount. But two thirds of sixty is forty thousand."

She smiled at him tantalizingly. "Is it a deal, Captain? Three ways. Twenty thousand for each of us."

"No."

The smile disappeared from her face and she came toward him. She came to within two feet of him and then looked up at him.

"We know things you don't know."

"I'll find them out."

"Will you? Are you so sure? Oh, the colonel's looked up your service record. It's very good. You've got more than the next man." She moistened her lips. "That's one of the reasons I—I mean, we, would like you with us, rather than against us. John . . ."

Her face bore a trace of crimson now. Slater was well aware of it and his hands, below her eye level, began to form fists.

"Yes?"

"Half."

He shook his head and her face turned a shade deeper. "I'm not very good at this," she said. "I—I haven't had much practice, but—but you can't be completely oblivious. You *must* know that there's a—a way you can get two thirds . . ."

"You mean . . . *like this?*"

He suddenly reached out and caught her in his arms and crushed her to him. Her face was turned up, her body was yielding and her lips, when his pressed down savagely, were responsive. And then her arms crept up and went about the back of his head. He kissed her hard and long and she returned it full measure. And then he released her and stepped back.

"I'm not interested in the money," he said hoarsely. "I don't want it. It's blood money."

She recoiled as if he had struck her.

"What *do* you want then?"

"The man who betrayed my father. The man who did to him . . . what was done . . ."

She stared at him a long moment, then a harsh laugh was torn from her throat. "You're a fool, John," she said. She turned from him and started to the door. She pulled it open, then stopped. "What do they say about a man back East when he's skipped town for some reason or another?"

"Why, that he's gone to Texas."

Susan smiled thinly. "That's right—gone to Texas. Well, a woman named Carson happens to live in Texas. The name mean anything—Helen Carson?" Susan stopped, smiled and went through the door.

Helen Carson. A Douglas Carson had been at Fort Starvation.

11

The road led to the west. It consisted of two winding ribbons, cut through the short buffalo grass. The driver of the first wagon team that had come this way had let his horses pick their way and those that came after that followed the trail, until now there was a well-defined road that turned out for a boulder or tree stump here and for a sloping knoll there.

The black gelding plodded between the two ruts. It walked with a peculiar, tired gait that seemed to have been transmitted to the man in the saddle. Slater rode completely relaxed and slumped forward so that his chin almost rested on his chest.

It was a wiltingly hot day, but he wore a coat, an alkali-stained, patched coat that was frayed at the cuffs. A flannel shirt, worn, faded levis and dusty, cracked boots, run down at the heels, completed his dress. Except for a flat-crowned black Stetson and a revolver that hung low on his right side, protruding beneath the coat.

Three miles back he had skirted the tiny hamlet of Broken Wagon. A man on the dodge would also skirt it and Slater was playing it safe.

The gelding lifted its head, whickered. Slater became alert. One moment there had been only a clump of cottonwoods ahead and to the left. Now two horsemen had materialized, sitting quietly in their saddles, rifles across pommels, pointed carelessly in his direction.

Slater pressed his knee into the gelding's side and it came to a stop thirty feet from the two horsemen. His halt encouraged the others to move their mounts forward into the rutted trail.

They were hard-looking men, one tall and heavy-set with a single revolver at his side, the other slight and hatchet faced, ugly and long nosed. Besides the rifle, he carried a gun at each thigh.

It was the big man who spoke. "Going far this way?"

Slater waited a moment before replying. "Not so far."

The answer didn't satisfy the big man. "To the hills?"

Slater shrugged.

The little man showed snaggled teeth. "Tough customer, hey?"

"Yes." It was a flat statement.

The little man seemed about to challenge Slater's assertion, but his companion shook his head slightly. He nodded to Slater. "Your name in the book?"

"What book?" Slater asked.

"Only one book'd have your name." The big man nodded. "You're headed for the hills. That means your name *is* in the book."

Slater gathered up the reins with his left hand. He knew when a fight could be avoided, just as well as when it had to be made.

He said, "I'm coming through . . ."

Their rifles were on him, they were two to one and he had only the one revolver. He had to carry the fight to them, smash or be smashed. He went for his gun, continued the downward movement, so all of his body but one leg was protected by the gelding. He fired under the animal's neck. It was a trick he had learned from his first sergeant, an old Indian fighter.

It should have been successful. That it wasn't was due entirely to the fact that the bigger man, instead of trying to snap shot with his rifle, reared his horse up on its hind legs. Slater's first bullet smashed into the animal's breasts, so that it screamed in anguish and plunged over backwards, unseating the big man.

Slater hadn't known, of course, that the little man was the

deadlier of the two. Because a man wore two guns didn't necessarily mean that he lived up to them. This one did. And it cost Slater the fight.

Before Slater could whip his revolver to the right, a bullet seared through the calf of his exposed leg and plowed deep into the black gelding's side. The animal broke in its plunge, stumbled and barely kept from falling. The stumble, more than the bullet, dislodged Slater. He landed heavily on one foot, fell to his knee, but, still gripping tight the bridle reins, let the gelding pull him up again.

He ran two or three steps beside the horse, then caught the pommel of his McClelland saddle and vaulted up. It was precision work. He touched the saddle and swiveled back, all in the same movement. The second rifle bullet caught him in the side.

This thing that was happening to her uncle was so new, so unlike him that Helen Carson could not understand it. She'd thought she'd known him. She'd been with him every day, since that day he had come riding to her grandmother's wearing a faded, patched gray uniform. She was fifteen then.

Major Carson was not a cheerful man. He had been with Joe Johnston at Bull Run, had followed him through the years, to North Carolina, where he had, with Johnston, tendered his sword to the gaunt, fierce-eyed Sherman.

The Yanks, the carpetbag politicians, ruled East Texas in 1865. Their attitude toward former officers of the Confederate Army was not conducive to a quiet, peaceful life, and Major Carson had taken his fifteen-year-old niece and headed westward, beyond the Pecos River where there were no settlements and no one to ask a man's political views.

There were men west of the Pecos, but they were furtive creatures who lived in the hills and sought anonymity. They asked no questions and wanted none asked of them. They came from all over the country. In the places where they had originated, officials had written after their names, "G.T.T."—Gone To Texas.

They had not bothered Major Carson when he had first come to the valley. Not ranchers themselves, they made no protest when he built a home and brought a herd of cattle to the valley. Perhaps they regretted not having discouraged him in the years that followed, but by that time Major Carson was

57

too firmly rooted in the valley and there were others like him, men whose cattle numbered in the thousands and roamed the broad valley at will.

After the ranchers came the farmers and small stockmen. They stopped their wagons one day and the next a shack or hut sprang seemingly out of the ground. They brought two or three horses with them, a cow or two, and broke the ground with their plows.

The big ranchers resented the invasion of the settlers. They made life miserable for them and gave them no rest. In the natural course of events they would have driven the little men westward or back toward the rising sun, from where they came. Except for one thing—spools of barbed wire that the ranchers brought out with them. It was the most devastating thing the ranchers had ever seen. The land did not belong to them, of course, except by right of conquest.

It was government land and every man had an equal right to it. The ranchers did not quarrel over the land, there was so much of it. If a settler here and there squatted on a quarter section, it was of no matter. The roaming herds of half-wild cattle trampled down anything the settlers planted. They broke down pole fences. But they did not break through the barbed wires that the little men strung around their farms. They did not break through the barbed wire, although they were sometimes thirsty and the wire enclosed a spring or waterhole.

Major Carson was the first rancher to settle in Broken Wagon Valley. That did not automatically make him the leader of the ranchers. He won that honor because he was the man most capable of accomplishing things. The other ranchers conceded that.

Helen Carson had seen the nesters come and had secretly welcomed them. There were women with them, girls her own age. Mary Holterman's father was a nester, yet Mary became Helen's best friend. She lived only two miles from the Carson ranch house and seldom a day passed that she did not ride over to visit Helen, or the latter go to see Mary.

Helen's uncle had not commented on the friendship until recently. And then, one day, he had announced that he did not want Helen to see Mary Holterman again. This morning, Helen had disobeyed her uncle. And when she returned

from the Holterman farm, her uncle had b⸻
on the veranda of the adobe ranch house. He sai⸻

"I told you not to see Mary Holterman again. I do ⸻
to remind you of that again."

In hurt astonishment, Helen had questioned: "But why, Uncle? Mary's my best friend. She's a fine girl and—"

"And her father's organizing the nesters to fight me," Major Carson snapped. He walked deliberately away from Helen, heading toward the corral behind the bunkhouse.

Helen watched him out of sight, stunned. Her chin trembled and she had to fight back the threatening tears. It was the first time he had ever used such a tone to her.

She was still standing there, staring toward the bunkhouse when Ambrose came out of the house. Ambrose had been a slave. Emancipation had freed him legally, but it had not changed his status with the Carson family, except that he asked for a dollar on the rare occasions when he went to the village of Broken Wagon.

He spoke softly to Helen. "Don't you bother, Miss Helen. The major got hisself a powerful lot of worry with them nesters. They fencin' in all the water."

Helen shook her head in bewilderment. "But there's room for everyone in the valley. The little ground the farmers are using doesn't amount to anything. They're all so poor—"

"They's white trash, Miss Helen," Ambrose said. "The major's right when he say you shouldn't ought to have no truck with them. Why don't you go take yourself a ride and get some of that fine sun? You'll feel better and when you come back I'll have lunch ready."

Helen did not particularly want to take a ride, but when Ambrose brought her saddled filly around in a few minutes she mounted it and started in the general direction of Broken Wagon some six miles from the ranch.

12

A mile from the ranch she saw the black gelding. It was standing beside the rutted road, bridle reins trailing. When Helen approached, the horse shied away but stopped a few paces beyond.

Then Helen saw the body on the ground, half concealed by a small clump of bushes. In a flash she was down on the ground, running forward. She had to part the bushes to see the upper half of the man's body and when she looked down and saw the blood-soaked clothes, she gasped aloud.

She was afraid to try to pull him out of the bushes, so she spent several moments bending down and breaking off branches. Finally she got in close and dropped to her knees.

He was lying on his back, his eyes closed, but he was alive and breathing, although only faintly. She did not think the wound in his leg was serious and paid no attention to it, but the blood-soaked shirt and coat caused her to shudder. She had seen wounds before; cowboys were always getting hurt, and the major generally acted as physician and surgeon. On several occasions Helen had been compelled to help him.

The wounded man weighed a hundred and seventy to one hundred and eighty pounds. Helen knew that she could never lift him to the saddle of her horse.

She drew back the tail of his coat, loosened his shirt and with her small, strong hands ripped it upwards, exposing the wound. It was still bleeding lightly and when Helen saw the wound she knew that the man was critically hurt.

She turned away, and lifting her riding skirt slightly, pulled down on her petticoat and tore into the hem five or six inches. Then calmly she began tearing the wide strip about the skirt. The petticoat was of good linen and the cloth would make a tight bandage. She fell again to her knees and putting both hands under the wounded man, turned him over on his side, so she could get the bandage under him.

She managed it, then put him back into his original position. As careful as she was, she must have hurt him, for a moan escaped his lips.

Her eyes darted to his face and she inhaled softly. His eyes were open and he was looking at her.

Scarlet flooded Helen's face and she bit her lip. Then she took hold of the bandage again. "You're badly hurt," she said. "I can't move you alone. I'm just going to fix this bandage, then I'll go for help. It won't take long."

She tore off a piece of the bandage, wadded it and placed it over the wound. Then she brought the two ends of the skirt hem together and tied them tightly, so the pad was pressed down on the wound.

Finally she got to her feet. "I won't be gone twenty minutes. Lie still until then."

His eyes blinked assent. Helen cried, "I'll hurry."

She stepped out of the bushes and ran toward the filly. Fortunately it did not pick this time to act coy and back away. She vaulted into the saddle and sent the animal galloping back toward the ranch.

In front of the ranch house she sprang from the saddle and ran toward the door, crying, "Ambrose! Get one of the men to hitch a team to the wagon. Put some blankets in it—and hurry."

Ambrose popped out of the house, his eyes rolling. "What's up, Miss Helen? Your uncle . . . ?"

"No-no, it's a stranger. He's up the road, badly hurt. We've got to bring him here. Hurry . . ."

From the doorway a cool voice said, "Easy, Amby."

Helen flashed a look at her uncle's foreman. Ned McTammany was thirty, a tall, broad-shouldered man, burned to the complexion of an Apache. His lips were curled perpetually into an insolent sneer. He could get twice the work out of the hands that Major Carson did.

He went on, "Who's this that's hurt, Helen?"

Helen exclaimed impatiently. "Get the wagon, Ambrose. And don't forget the blankets." When Ambrose had trotted off, she turned to the foreman. "A stranger. I found him up the road. He's been shot."

"A stranger? Shot?" McTammany sniffed. "One of the wild bunch from the hills? Let him lie where he is."

"What?" cried Helen. "Why—why, he's seriously hurt. He'll die!"

"What if he does? They're always fighting among themselves up there. We don't want to have anything to do with them. Let them kill each other off."

Anger drove the color from Helen Carson's face. "Ned McTammany, that's the most cold-blooded thing I've ever heard. He's been badly wounded, he's dying."

"Your uncle would let him die," McTammany said sullenly. "He's told me over and over not to mix with the bunch in the hills."

"Here comes Ambrose with the wagon," Helen said coldly. "You can stay here if you want, but Ambrose . . . !"

McTammany suddenly sprang from the veranda and bounded into the body of the wagon. He reached forward and jerked the lines from the Negro's hands.

"I'll drive!"

13

Slater opened his eyes and looked at the clean, whitewashed ceiling above him. Then he dropped his eyes and saw the white walls around him and finally the blankets and sheets that covered him.

He stirred and dull pain touched his left side, the calf of his left leg. He lay still, reviewing the events that preceded his lapse into unconsciousness.

He'd encountered two hard-looking men on the trail who had disputed his right to pass. He'd shot it out with them—and they had beaten him.

Or had they? He remembered now that he had fled down the trail, that he had fallen from his horse and lain for some time in semiconsciousness, until he had opened his eyes and looked into the scared, white face of a girl.

A step sounded just outside the door of the bedroom and then the door opened. A lean, middle-aged man looked in, saw that Slater's eyes were open and came into the room. He closed the door carefully behind him.

"You've come round."

Slater blinked assent and kept his eyes on the other's face. Major Carson said, "I'm Major Carson. My niece had you brought here—yesterday." He looked thoughtfully at Slater, then nodded. "Your name's in the book?"

The book. Those men yesterday had asked practically the same question.

"What book?"

"The Crime Book. The adjutant-general got it out six months ago. It's got eight thousand names in it."

"As far as I know," Slater said deliberately, "my name isn't in *any* book."

"The Crime Book," Major Carson went on, "has the names of all known criminals believed to be within the borders of Texas. Those men you had the fight with, they were here last night. They're coming again today. They're Rangers. They haven't admitted it, but I know."

"One of those men has a hatchet face?" Slater asked.

"That's the one who calls himself Johnny Buff. But the big man Welker's the leader."

Welker might be the leader, Slater thought, but the little man, Buff, was the dangerous one of the two. Not that Welker wasn't bad enough, but Buff was infinitely more so. It was he who had bested Slater.

Rangers? They had a strange breed of law officers in Texas. Slater said, "My clothes . . ."

Major Carson grunted. "You think you can get up and ride on into the hills? Uh-uh, not for quite a spell."

"I've got to."

"You only killed Welker's horse," Major Carson snorted. "How were you to know they weren't from the hills? They didn't *say* they were Rangers, did they?"

"I don't know that they *are* Rangers."

"Oh, they are, all right. The boys in the hills never come down here. They're McNeilly's boys. The only reason they're not in the hills themselves is that they've got jobs and they're wearing badges. They're killers, every last one of them. And McNeilly's the worst of them all. He hasn't arrested six men in the last six months, but they say a thousand men have disappeared in that time. Well, maybe they deserved it, but making the Rangers paid murderers don't help matters any. . . . You stay here. I'll give you a job."

Slater blinked in surprise. "Me? A job?"

"If you go for the hills you'll never return. This is your chance to rehabilitate yourself. And besides, I need men like you. I'm in the middle of a—I mean, I don't trust my foreman, Ned McTammany, any further than I could throw a Longhorn. I need——"

Carson stopped. The door opened suddenly and Helen

Carson's blonde head poked into the room. Her eyes lit up when she saw Slater was conscious.

"You're awake. Good. Uncle, you shouldn't——"

"We've been talking. Uh . . ." He looked inquiringly at Slater. "You've met my niece?"

"I owe you my thanks——"

Helen Carson cut him off. "What else could I do? You were wounded . . ."

"My name," said Slater carefully, "is John Slater."

It made no impression on either Major Carson or his niece. He looked steadily into the major's eyes a moment, then let his lids flutter and half close, as if in fatigue. Instantly Helen Carson exclaimed, "We'd better let him rest, Uncle!"

They left the room. Slater's eyes drifted to a door at the side of the room. A closet. His clothing was probably in there.

He threw back the blankets and swung his feet outward, to put them on the floor. He did not immediately complete the movement, for a spasm of pain exploded in his side and filtered to every part of his body, almost blinding him.

For a moment he fought nausea, then won out, rose and crossed the room. His shabby clothing hung in the closet. They had even put his Navy Colt in with the clothing. He dressed, buckled the cartridge belt about his waist.

He crossed to the door leading out of the bedroom. As he touched the knob he heard loud voices outside.

One of the voices said, "His horse is in the corral. It's been shot. You've got him here and we want him."

Major Carson's voice said warmly, "No man takes another out of my house without my permission."

Welker's voice sneered, "A bloody king, ain't you? A cattle king who's master of all he surveys. Well, I'm Sergeant Welker of the Texas Rangers. The State of Texas is talking when I talk. Step aside, Mister or . . ."

Slater opened the door and stepped through. "Here I am, Welker."

Johnny Buff was also in the room.

Major Carson saw Slater and exclaimed, "John, you shouldn't have got up."

Slater made a slight brushing gesture. His eyes remained on Welker. "What do you want with me?"

"I don't want anything with you," retorted Welker. "I want you."

"You've got a warrant for me?"

Welker took a nickeled badge from his shirt pocket. "That's my warrant. If your name's in the Crime Book——"

"It isn't."

"What's your name?" Welker took a well-thumbed little booklet from his pocket.

"Slater, John Slater."

Welker quickly thumbed through the pages of the little book, showed disappointment. He looked inquiringly at Johnny Buff. The latter shook his head.

"I've only got your word that Slater *is* your name." He scowled. "Besides, you pulled a gun on me. Killed my horse."

Major Carson exclaimed, "How the devil was he to know you weren't an outlaw? You certainly don't look like a law man."

Welker bared his teeth. "Look, Carson, I've been hearing things about you. Lots of things. You think you're God Almighty Himself. No one around here's bothered to trim your horns. But that's all over. We're moving in here and I'm telling you right now that the things you've been getting away with won't go any more. I represent the State of Texas——"

"You represent a small political faction who happen to be running things in Austin," Major Carson snapped. "Out here you don't represent anything. I'm telling you, don't try anything. With me or anyone working for me."

Johnny Buff spoke up suddenly. "Slater working for you?"

"He is."

Welker continued doggedly, "He killed my horse."

"Sue him, then! And now, good morning. We've got work to do around here."

Johnny Buff shrugged and started for the door. Welker held his ground a moment, but finally followed Buff outside. Major Carson exhaled heavily as he turned to Slater.

"You shouldn't have got out of bed, Slater."

"I'm all right," Slater said. "I've got to be going. Those fellows aren't going to let this drop."

"What can they do? There're only two of them. The local sheriff knows which side his bread is buttered. He isn't going to back up a couple of gun hawks who happen to be wearing badges given them by someone five hundred miles away."

"They're the law. If they fail there'll be others coming after them."

"Not here. Why, out there in the hills are hundreds of men who've been here for years and no one's bothered them. Thieves, highwaymen, killers. There aren't enough Rangers in Texas to drive those men out of the hills. And there aren't enough to come into this valley and run things. No, there's no danger from the Rangers. Not from them."

"From who then?" Slater asked.

Major Carson's face twisted. "From the people here in the valley. The nesters and the sodbusters. We let them come in and now they outnumber us. They're crowding us off the range with their fences. They're letting our cattle die of thirst by fencing in waterholes." The Major noted Slater's speculative look. "All right, I'll put it to you bluntly. There's been trouble and there'll be more of it. That's why I want you to work for me."

"You've put it bluntly," said Slater. "So I'll give it back to you in the same way. You're not hiring me, you're hiring my gun."

"That *is* putting it bluntly."

Slater said, "All right, I'll stay—awhile. If I can get a little rest."

"Of course. You ought to be in bed right now."

"If you don't mind, I'd like to sit out in the sun awhile."

The major stepped quickly to the door, opened it and turned to help Slater. But Slater shook his head and walked out unaided.

There was a wicker armchair on the veranda. Slater sat down heavily in it and looked out over the peaceful ranch yard. Major Carson stopped on the veranda a moment, then walked out toward the corrals.

Slater sat there ten minutes or so, when he heard boots crunch the hard-packed earth and Ned McTammany came around the corner of the house.

The tall foreman's face twisted inscrutably when he saw Slater. "I'm Ned McTammany, the foreman," he said. "The major just told me that you're going to stay on awhile."

"I suppose I ought to move over to the bunkhouse?"

The foreman shook his head. "No hurry. The boss says

you're to stay in the house until you get feeling better. Uh, I was with the girl when she picked you up. Tough. . . ."

McTammany stopped, looked closely at Slater. "Your name's Slater, isn't it?"

"Yes." Slater finally gave the lean foreman his attention.

But McTammany nodded affably, moved on with, "See you around, Slater."

14

For five days Slater occupied the comfortable chair on the veranda of the Carson ranch house, from seven in the morning until seven in the evening, leaving it only for meals inside. He soaked up the heat until the soreness went out of his body.

In midmorning of the sixth day, Helen Carson came out of the house. She was wearing boots, a riding skirt and carried a small crop.

"I think I'll take a ride this morning," she said to Slater. "It's a good day for it."

Helen half started off the veranda, hesitated. Something was on her mind.

Slater said, "Ever hear of a man named Al Johnston?"

"There's a Johnston lives near Broken Wagon," Helen replied. "But I think his first name is Henry, not Al."

"How old a man is he?"

"Forty, forty-five. He's got four children, the oldest a boy named Hank, around twenty."

"I don't think this'd be the same Johnston."

Helen regarded him curiously. "I thought you were a stranger in this section?"

"I am. Just happened to hear of this Al Johnston. Supposed to be somewhere around this area." Slater looked at her thoughtfully. "How old were you when your father died?"

"Eight or nine. I scarcely remember him."

"Your mother's told you about him, though."

"My mother? She died when I was born. I lived with my grandmother until Uncle Raymond returned from the war." Helen looked sharply at Slater. But Slater looked out toward the corrals.

"While your father was still alive, did he live with you and your grandmother?"

"He came to visit us once every year or two." Helen's eyes remained on Slater's averted face. "I remember him as a big man with a huge yellow mustache. His name was Douglas and he came to Texas from Tennessee right after the Mexican War. In fact, he served here during the war, liked the country and returned afterwards. Now, are there any other little details you'd like to know about my family?"

Slater could no longer avoid the irony in her tone. He looked at her. "Excuse me for prying. I was almost certain I'd met your father. There was a man named Doug Carson I met in '62. He was from Texas."

"It couldn't have been my father. He died in 1861."

"In Texas?"

"In Utah. He was one of a party of prospectors who were killed by Indians. And now, if you don't mind, I think I'll take that ride." She nodded coolly to him, strode out toward the corrals.

Slater watched her start off her horse, headed in an easterly direction.

Some ten minutes later, Ambrose came out of the house. Slater got to his feet, stretched.

"How's my horse, Ambrose?"

"Fit as a colt. He didn't have on'y a scratch. You—you wasn't thinkin' of ridin' him already?"

"If you'll find my saddle."

Ambrose's face creased. "Major won't like that. He say you still purty sick."

"I'm well enough. I'd like you to get my horse."

Ambrose hesitated, then headed out for the corrals, shaking his head. In a few minutes he returned, leading Slater's gelding, saddled.

Slater climbed stiffly into the saddle and turned the gelding's head to the north. The animal trotted off briskly and

70

Slater winced as the jolting reached his wounds. He pulled the horse up to a walk.

Cresting a knoll a half mile from the Carson ranch house, Slater looked down into a shallow ravine that was studded with cottonwood trees and in the center a thick growth of brush.

He caught a glimpse of a bay horse being pulled into the thicket of brush as he started down the slope into the ravine. He let his bridle reins fall carelessly and dropped his hands to his sides.

When the gelding entered the cottonwoods, Slater made a quick movement with his left leg, swinging it over the pommel and in the same motion dropping lightly to the ground. His right hand whipped out his Navy Colt and peering into the brush, he called:

"All right, come out!"

For a moment there was silence and Slater wondered if the answer to his challenge would be a bullet. Then the bushes parted and a scared face appeared, the face of a girl.

She stepped free of the bushes and Slater's eyes narrowed. She was an amazingly pretty girl; she wore levis and boots, a flannel shirt but no hat, her hair hanging in two chestnut braids down her back.

Slater slipped his Colt back into its holster. "Who are you?" he asked the girl.

"Mary Holterman. I live back there." She jerked a thumb over her shoulder. Then she smiled pertly at Slater. "Who're you?"

"My name's John Slater."

"Oh yes, the gunman."

Slater winced. "Why were you hiding here in the brush?"

"I wasn't—I mean, I wasn't hiding." Her nose wrinkled as the sudden clop-clop of a horse's hoofs came over. Slater's hand went automatically to his gun, but he let the hand fall again as he caught a glimpse of the new arrival. It was Helen Carson.

She didn't see him until she was almost in the bushes. Then she pulled up her horse sharply and looked at him with hostile eyes.

"Hello," Slater said. "I was just taking a little ride."

"Well," she said in a brittle tone, "you know now. I suppose you'll make your report to my uncle."

"Why would I do that?"

Mary Holterman answered for Helen Carson. "Just because my father and Helen's uncle don't get along is no reason for *us* to be enemies, Mr. Slater. I was waiting here for Helen."

Slater stared at the two girls in astonishment. "You mean you two have to meet secretly?"

"Uncle hasn't told you?" Helen Carson demanded. "Then how did you happen to be here?"

"I chose this direction quite by accident."

"I'll bet!"

Slater nodded stiffly, turned his horse and left the two girls in the brush. He rode ahead, down the ravine.

When he reached the far crest of the ravine, Slater could see the Holterman ranch, a squat adobe house, a barn and a pole corral. And straight ahead of Slater, between him and the ranch buildings was something Slater had never seen before. A barbed wire fence.

Slater rode up to the fence and leaning over, examined the sharp barbs. Yes, they would tear a steer's hide all right. They would——

ZING!

A bullet whined over Slater's head and almost instantly the bang of a high-powered rifle smote his ears. Before the report had died out, Slater's Navy Colt was in his fist, cocked.

But he held his fire. A tall, heavy-set man, carrying a Sharp's rifle, strode toward Slater from the red adobe house. He yelled when still some distance away.

"Don't you cut that wire!"

Slater straightened in the saddle. "I wasn't going to cut it," he called back. "I was just looking at it."

"Looking, hell!" retorted Amos Holterman. He approached steadily. "I got a notion to take you to Broken Wagon and turn you over to the sheriff. It's time we called a showdown on this wire-cutting business."

Holterman seemed oblivious of the revolver in Slater's hand, or else he had the sublime confidence of the rancher that the rifle was a superior weapon to the Navy revolver.

Slater said easily, "This is the first time I've seen barbed wire."

"Yah!" jeered Holterman. "You're one of Carson's men,

72

ain't you? He's been hirin' gunslingers. Nick Fedderson was seen in town last week."

"Who's Nick Fedderson?"

Holterman looked at him wide-eyed. "You really try your damnedest, don't you? The whole State of Texas knows that Nick Fedderson's the leader of the wild bunch up in the hills, but you—you never even heard of him."

"I haven't."

"That's as far as I go with you. You're probably one of Nick's men. I've said enough. Now, throw down that wire cutter."

"I haven't got a wire cutter. I've never even seen barbed wire until today."

"I've said all I've got to say," Holterman said ominously. "Now throw down that peashooter. I'm going to teach you a little lesson. A lesson that maybe'll keep some of Nick Fedderson's boys from comin' down here." He gestured with the rifle. "Throw the gun down. I mean it."

Slater didn't want to shoot the rancher and the man was making an issue of it. So it was shoot, or . . .

He dropped his gun.

The sound of galloping hoofs came up behind Slater. He shot a quick glance over his shoulder, saw that it was Mary Holterman coming up swiftly. Holterman saw his daughter, too, and coming forward, kicked Slater's gun aside.

"So you're a gun fighter, eh? And like all of them yellow when a man's gun is pointing at you."

Mary Holterman pulled up her horse, bounced to the ground. "Father!" she exclaimed. "Put down your gun."

"Go to the house," snapped Holterman. "Saddle my horse and bring him here. I'm going to take this wire cutter to Broken Wagon and turn him over to the sheriff."

"You can't, Father. This man works for Major Carson."

"That's why I'm going to have him arrested."

"Please, Father," pleaded Mary Holterman. "You mustn't make trouble. I—I'm sure he didn't intend to cut the wire."

His daughter's plea was so earnest that Amos Holterman began to waver. "We've got to make an issue of this sooner or later. Carson can't keep cutting our wire." He made a sudden impatient gesture of surrender. "All right, Slater, turn your horse and get the devil away from here. But I'm warning you, don't you come near my fence again. Understand?"

Slater gestured to the gun on the ground. Holterman shook his head. "I don't trust any man from Carson's place. You can call for your gun at Sheriff Wagner's office in Broken Wagon. Git now!"

15

Slater was again seated on the veranda of the Carson ranch house the next morning when Major Carson came in from the range. He clumped onto the veranda, looked down at Slater. "Sixteen steers with their hides torn by wire," he said savagely. "And eight of them shot. I'm going in to Broken Wagon to call for a showdown."

"Mind if I ride into town with you?"

"It's five miles."

"I can make it. I want to get a few things."

"All right, if you think you won't be overdoing it. Mmm, Helen's going in with us."

The three of them rode easily into Broken Wagon. Slater looked now and then at Helen, but she remained close to her uncle's side. He caught her eyes on him once, but she averted them. She hadn't spoken to him since the day before, was apparently determined not to.

There were perhaps seventy-five buildings in the town of Broken Wagon, all on the one short street. Six of the buildings were saloons. Major Carson headed for the hitchrail in front of Hackberry's General Store.

"Do your shopping while I run over to the sheriff's office," Major Carson told his niece. He looked at Slater. "A half hour enough for you?"

"Yes."

The major nodded, headed across the street.

Slater finished tying his horse to the hitchrail, turned to Helen. She had completed the task of tying her own horse, was looking steadily at him when his eyes met hers.

"Who are you?" she demanded bluntly.

Slater looked at her sharply. "My name's Slater, John Slater."

"That's what you said before, but you also said you were a stranger in these parts. And yesterday you asked me a lot of questions about my family. And—somebody *else* has been asking about me. Somebody who knows you."

"Who?"

Helen made an impatient gesture of dismissal. "You're hired out to Uncle Raymond as a gun fighter."

Slater moved closer to Helen. "Who is it knows me?"

"I'm not telling you anything any more. Not until I get some straight answers about you."

Slater's eyes narrowed. "You met the Holterman girl yesterday. So you heard some things from her. What?"

"When you get ready to talk, I'll talk." Helen's eyes blazed. She whirled away and strode to the door of the general store.

Slater looked after her, then turned and crossed the street to the sheriff's office.

As he reached the door, Major Carson's voice come angrily from inside. "I don't give a damn what you say, Wagner. My steers are being mutilated and killed and I'm not going to stand for it any more."

"Now, Major," said the sheriff. "Maybe the damage ain't all on your side. The farmers have been takin' a lot of punishment from havin' their wire cut and crops trampled. On'y yesterday Amos Holterman came in to complain about one of your men cuttin' his wire."

"That's a lie!" burst out Major Carson. "I've given my men strict orders, time and again, to leave the wire alone. None of them would dare——"

"No? Well, it happens that Holterman caught your man red handed. Took away his gun."

Slater pushed open the door and went into the office. "Sheriff Wagner?" he asked. "I understand you have a gun belonging to me?"

Wagner was a burly, red-faced man crowding fifty. He blinked at Slater. "What gun?"

"A Navy Colt. Amos Holterman said he was going to turn it over to you."

Major Carson gasped. "You!"

"See?" cried the sheriff triumphantly. "What did I tell you?"

"Slater, *you* didn't cut his wire!"

"Of course not. I'd never seen barbed wire before. I stopped to look at it and that's when Holterman——"

"Yah!" jeered the sheriff.

Major Carson whirled on the sheriff. "You damn fool, he's telling the truth. He's new to this country. Just came here last week."

Slater said, "Do you mind giving me my gun?"

Sheriff Wagner pulled open the drawer of a desk and brought out Slater's Navy Colt. He slid it across the scarred wood and said significantly to Major Carson, "Do you still want to make that complaint?"

Major Carson cast a bitter glance at Slater and, without a word, turned on his heel. Slater slipped his revolver into its holster.

Carson was waiting for Slater outside. "Slater," he said thickly, "how did Holterman come to take your gun away from you?"

"He threw down on me with a rifle."

"And you let him?"

"I would have had to kill him. I didn't want to do that."

"Holterman's the leader of the nesters." Major Carson stared at Slater. "And you didn't want to kill him. Oh, hell!"

Carson snorted and started across the dirt street. Slater looked toward the near-by saloon and went to it. He entered and ordered a glass of beer.

It was cool and refreshing and he drank it slowly. Ned McTammany, who was standing at the far end of the bar, came over.

"Hello, Slater," he said. "Kind of a long trip for you, ain't it?"

Slater shrugged. McTammany's face twisted into a cruel grin. "I guess you got some practice yesterday. Hear you were out riding—over toward Holterman's place." He looked pointedly at the gun in Slater's holster.

Slater said deliberately, "Look, McTammany, I don't like you either. You want to let it rest there, or . . . ?"

McTammany still grinned, but the grin was frozen on his lips. He said, "I'll let it rest—for now."

Slater walked out of the saloon.

As he came through the doors, he almost collided with Amos Holterman. Holterman's eyes lit up and he grabbed Slater's arm.

"Just the man I've been lookin' for," he exclaimed. "I want to apologize about yesterday. I—I found out that you *are* new to this country and probably hadn't seen barbed wire before."

Slater's eyes went past Holterman. Getting out of a buckboard were Mary Holterman and Susan Orpington. Susan was wearing a blue gingham dress.

Her eyes were on him and she was smiling.

"Hello!"

Holterman half turned, grinned. "Neighbors from back home. Alf Orpington and his daughter, Sue. Your name came up and Sue said she'd seen you in Kansas on'y a few weeks ago."

"You're from Kansas?" Slater asked.

"Uh-uh, Illinois. Sangamon County. The Orpingtons hail from there originally."

Slater nodded, moved toward the buckboard.

"Kind of sudden, your visit here?" he said to Susan Orpington.

"Why, no, not at all. And it isn't exactly a visit. We—Father and I have been planning to move out here for some time and when we heard that some Sangamon County people had settled here———"

Holterman interrupted. "I see you've got your gun from the sheriff, Slater. Guess I'd better drop in on him and square things."

He smiled, nodded and hurried off toward the sheriff's office. Mary Holterman climbed down from the buckboard. "If you don't mind, Susan, I'll run across to the store."

"I'll join you there in a minute," Susan Orpington said.

Mary Holterman went off and Slater moved closer to the buckboard. "You're *sure* you're from Sangamon County, Illinois?"

"Prove that we aren't," Susan smiled tantalizingly. "You wouldn't be here if I hadn't tipped you off about the Carsons.

78

All right, you've moved in with them, we've moved in with the Holtermans——"

"Who happened to be the leaders of the faction opposed to Major Carson."

"I've heard there's no love lost between Holterman and Carson."

"Have you also heard that a range war's about ready to break out?"

Susan shrugged. "*I'm* not interested in range wars." She started to get down from the buckboard, waited for Slater to help her. He did. She smiled her thanks.

"What have you found out so far?"

"Nothing."

She looked at him sharply. "That's not like you." She nodded suddenly. "You're going to keep things to yourself."

"I just told you all that I've found out so far. That's nothing."

"Didn't the name Slater register with Major Carson?"

"If it did, he didn't let on. He hasn't questioned me. I'm a professional gunhand to him, that's all."

"You were shot by a Texas Ranger."

"You've heard that? They gave me my reputation."

Amos Holterman came out of the sheriff's office, started back toward the buckboard. Across the street, Major Carson came out of the general store and started across the street. Then he saw Holterman. He stopped in his tracks.

Holterman caught sight of Carson, started toward him.

"Carson," he called, "I want to have a talk with you . . ."

Major Carson reached for his gun. Holterman saw the movement, threw up his hand. "Carson, wait. . . !"

Carson's gun appeared, roared. The bullet missed Holterman by three feet. Then Holterman's gun spoke. Carson cried out, fell to his knees.

Slater swore under his breath, ran out into the street. He passed Holterman, who was standing, his gun lowered, a look of horror and astonishment on his face.

"I didn't mean to," he began.

Major Carson was still on his knees, bracing himself on his hands. Blood was staining the right leg of his trousers. As Slater's boots pounded up, Carson twisted up his face.

"Slater," he said thickly, "get out of my sight before I kill you."

Helen Carson, with Mary Holterman behind her, came running up from the general store. "Get away from him," she cried to Slater. "Get away from him, you—you murderer!"

She dropped to her knees beside her uncle, sobbing.

Slater turned and walked to his horse. As he mounted, he saw Susan Orpington running toward him. But he turned his horse away from her and rode out of the town.

16

A week ago Slater had been riding toward the hills. His eyes had been so intent on them that he had scarely been aware of the green valley through which he passed. His eyes were only on the hills ahead. They were bleak and forbidding. They seemed to have been created by a gigantic hand that had torn up huge handfuls of earth and rock and tossed them down willynilly, as if in anger or spite. There was no rhyme or sense to it. Gullies ran here and there, as often as not ended against blind walls of rock.

There was, however, a trail of sorts leading into the badlands. Slater gave his gelding its head and the animal picked its way alone.

A man stepped out from behind a huge boulder. He was a whiskered, evil-looking individual in ragged clothes, but carried a fine repeating Winchester in his hands.

"That'll be far enough, Mister," he said to Slater.

Slater said, "I'm looking for Nick Fedderson."

"Why?"

Slater looked at the rifleman intently but made no reply. After a moment the other man shrugged. "All right, go ahead, but if you want to see Nick, make a lot of noise. It'll be healthier for you."

It was good advice and as Slater rode on he kept the gelding on rocky ground. A half mile past the first lookout, he was stopped again, this time by two men who had horses grazing near by. They mounted their animals and followed Slater closer as he went on.

After another mile there was a third challenge, but Slater was allowed to proceed. He topped a rocky rise in the trail and suddenly looked down upon a tight little valley of no more than eight or ten acres in area. A dozen crude shacks built of logs were scattered about the valley and at least twenty-five or thirty men were loafing around.

One of Slater's escort pulled up beside him. "Better start thinking up answers."

Slater's approach was watched with interest by the man in the valley. Slater picked out the largest group, gathered in front of the best cabin.

A man sprawled in a chair made of canvas and poles. He was lean faced, hawk eyed, with drooping mustaches that almost concealed a cruel mouth. He was about forty.

Slater dismounted before the hawk-eyed man, calmly squatted himself on the ground. The man in the chair studied him for seconds, then finally snapped, "Well?"

"My name's John Slater."

Nick Fedderson regarded Slater dourly. "I been expectin' you. You can climb on your horse and get the hell out of here."

Slater remained seated on the ground. Fedderson bared stained teeth. "You heard me. You've got McNeilly's Rangers after you as well as the crowd out in the valley. I don't want you here."

Slater said, "I think I'll stay."

Fedderson half rose from his chair but dropped back as Slater's hand moved closer to his right thigh. Fedderson stared at him, then half turned.

"Luke!"

A man who had been sprawled on the ground a short distance away got to his feet and sauntered over. He was a slender, clean-shaven man in his late twenties and carried a single Colt revolver stuck in the waistband of his trousers.

"This is John Slater, Luke," Fedderson said. "The man who had the run-in with McNeilly's boys. Slater, this is Luke Vickers. You heard of him?"

"No," Slater said.

Luke Vickers smiled thinly. "I never heard of you either. Those Rangers aren't so much. Anyway, they downed you."

"So?"

Fedderson and Vickers exchanged glances. Vickers said, "He don't scare me."

Fedderson nodded thoughtfully. "He don't seem scared either." He turned to Slater. "You can stay, Slater. There's just one thing you got to remember. Nick Fedderson runs things in these hills."

"That suits me," Slater replied coolly. "I never cared about running things anyway."

Fedderson nodded. "Things ain't like they used to be. Hell, man, I was here before the war. We never saw anyone then from one month to the next. I made a mistake lettin' the ranchers settle outside. At first I thought it was easy pickin's. Plenty of beef, a few dollars once in a while. But now, dammit, the valley's full of people and you can't tell who's a spy for McNeilly and who isn't. For all I know you might be one."

"That's true, you don't know, Fedderson. I might have let Buff and Welker put a slug in me just to get a chance to throw in with you."

Fedderson frowned. "Uh-uh, they tried to down you, all right. They come around to get you afterwards." He shrugged. "I ain't tellin' you nothing, Slater, nothing you couldn't figure out for yourself. Of course, I'm getting information from the valley. Be a fool if I wasn't."

"I don't figure you for a fool," Slater said.

Fedderson's eyes were suddenly looking past Slater. Slater got to his feet, turned. A single rider was coming down the rocky trail into the valley. He was coming at a pretty good clip and the fact that he was alone told Slater that he was one of Fedderson's crew.

"Moynahan," Vickers observed after a moment.

Fedderson nodded. The attention of the outlaws remained on the approaching rider, until Moynahan pulled up his horse in a cloud of dust and sprang to the ground.

Fedderson got up from his chair and moved forward. "You been ridin' hard."

Moynahan nodded. "McNeilly's moving into Broken Wagon with a company of Rangers."

"How many men?"

"They say a hundred. Word is that he's coming because of the range war the ranchers have started against the nesters."

"He doesn't need a hundred Rangers for that," Luke Vickers observed.

"He's coming because of us," Fedderson said. He drew a great breath and exhaled slowly. "Well, I can't say that I haven't been expectin' it. That's why I made my plans."

"Plans, Nick?" Vickers asked.

"Mexico. Old Juarez has got his hands full down there and he isn't going to bother much about a bunch of gringos who come down there, especially if the gringos got their pockets full of gold."

"What gold?" Vickers laughed.

Fedderson looked steadily at Vickers, then shifted to Slater. "The gold we're going to take with us. Like I told you, I've seen this comin' and I made my plans. I'd been afraid maybe McNeilly would get here too soon, but he hasn't. I closed the deal yesterday. The man's coming tomorrow with the gold." He moistened his lips. "The down payment on twenty-five thousand head of steers."

Slater controlled an involuntary start, but Vickers exclaimed aloud, "Twenty-five thousand steers!"

"At thirty dollars a head. Three quarters of a million. And all we have to do is deliver the steers across the river."

"Who," asked Slater, "is going to buy twenty-five thousand steers?"

Fedderson chuckled. "Not that it's any of your business, Slater, but it happens to be a country somewhere in the West Indies. Their agent discovered that steers would cost him sixty dollars apiece delivered in New Orleans. He figured he'd rather pay twenty-five dollars apiece delivered across the river. He can drive them to Vera Cruz and ship from there and save about thirty dollars a head."

"Which he'll put in his own pocket!"

Fedderson shrugged. "That's no affair of mine. He pays us one hundred thousand dollars in gold tomorrow and the balance when we deliver across the river."

"Only one thing wrong with that scheme," interposed Luke Vickers. "We ain't got twenty-five thousand steers. We ain't got even one steer."

"The game's played out here, Luke. There's no place left to go but Mexico. I figure the boys would like to go to Mexico with gold in their jeans." He turned to Slater. "What do you think?"

"It smells, Fedderson. I'm not in on it."

"Wrong, Slater. You *are* in it. Everyone in the hills is in it. If you don't believe me, stick around here after we're gone and see if you can convince McNeilly that you had nothing to do with it."

"You know what I think, Fedderson," Slater said slowly. "You're a little crazy."

Fedderson bared his teeth. "I've been on the dodge fifteen years, Slater. I'm still around." He nodded to Luke. "Send some boys down the trail. Nobody gets down the road from now on. Understand?"

Vickers nodded, trotted off to a saddled horse. He mounted and rode toward the mountain trail. Fedderson turned to Slater. "I want a word with you."

Slater followed him to one side, out of earshot of the other outlaws. "I got a report on you, Slater . . ."

"From Ned McTammany?"

"All right, from McTammany."

"I thought he was in with you."

"I've got a half dozen men out in the valley. Had to have them. The point is, I don't trust anyone. Not even Luke Vickers. You had a fight with Welker and Buff. From what I hear it was a sure-enough fight, but then you hired out to Carson as a gunfighter and threw down your gun to a sodbuster. Why?"

"I would have had to kill him otherwise."

"You'd rather be killed than kill? That ain't what I figure you for. You been asking for a man named Al Johnston?"

"Where'd you hear that?"

"It's true, isn't it?"

Slater regarded Fedderson thoughtfully. "You know Al Johnston?"

"A name don't mean a thing here in the hills. Any one of these men could be Al Johnston. How would I know?"

"I guess you wouldn't."

"Why do you want Johnston?"

"That's a personal matter."

"Is it?"

"It's got nothing to do with you . . . unless you happen to be Al Johnston yourself."

17

All day long, Major Carson sat on the veranda, his wounded leg propped up on a stool. His eyes stared straight ahead out over his bunkhouses and corrals, his vast rangeland, but he saw nothing of what he was looking at.

Helen Carson came and went during the day, but did not stop to talk to her uncle. There was no use as long as he was in such a frame of mind. He had to think it out for himself, decide whether or not she had betrayed him. He was convinced that the men who were responsible for his condition were John Slater and Amos Holterman; Slater, whom he had befriended, and Holterman from whom he had suffered because of the friendship of the two girls.

Carson had forbidden his niece to see Mary Holterman. She had disobeyed him and by that act of disobedience betrayed him. The hand behind Holterman's gun had been his niece's.

Ambrose came out at noon and informed the major that his lunch was ready. Carson waved him away.

Ned McTammany came later to tell him about a couple of steers that had torn themselves on the barbed wire and Carson merely stared coldly at him until McTammany went away, muttering to himself.

Dinnertime came and Ambrose set the table as usual, put food on it. Helen Carson sat down to the meal and could not eat. She pushed back her chair, went out to the veranda.

"It's no good, Uncle," she said. "We've got to talk this out."

"There's nothing to talk about."

"There's a lot to talk about. You're blaming me——"

"I'm blaming myself."

"No, you're not. You think because Mary Holterman and I were friends——"

"I told you not to see her."

"Who else was there for me to see? Don't you see, Uncle Raymond, I've lived here with you for years. I've seen only men, cowhands. I haven't known a girl, a woman since we came out here. I never knew my mother. You've refused even to talk about her."

"There's nothing I could tell you about her. She was my sister, but she married a good-for-nothing scoundrel. A handsome man like this Slater—and just as worthless."

"But Mother loved him."

"Women always love this kind. I hate to say this to you, Helen, but your father was just like—like this John Slater."

Helen Carson took a step closer to her uncle. "You think I'm in love with John Slater?"

"Are you?"

"No. But—but I want to talk to you about him. He asked me a lot of questions, questions that have been bothering me. About my father."

Major Carson sat up straighter. "What kind of questions?"

"How he died . . . and where?"

"What did you tell him?"

"Only what you told me. That he'd been killed by Indians in Utah."

"That was the report I got . . ." But suddenly Major Carson's eyes narrowed. "Slater. I thought the name was familiar, but it's been so long that——"

From the west came distant, rapid gunfire. Both Helen and the major turned.

"It's up in the hills," Helen said.

"No, it's closer. Get Ned McTammany!"

Startled by the sudden sharpness of her uncle's tone, Helen whirled and ran toward the bunkhouses. It was suppertime for the hands and most of them were in the mess shack, where a Chinese cooked for the hands. But McTammany was not there.

"Where's Ned McTammany?" Helen asked the group at large.

"Ain't seen him all afternoon," one of the hands replied.

"He said somethin' about checkin' on the stock in the west section," another man offered.

Helen ran out of the mess shack, back to her uncle. "McTammany isn't here. Is there—is there anything I can do?"

Major Carson groaned. "Something's happening. There's more dust over there in the west than there has a right to be, without any wind to speak of. And too much shooting. Damn this leg." He started to get up, groaned and dropped back in his chair.

But then the galloping of a horse's hoofs caused Helen to turn. It was Ned McTammany, coming at a gallop—from the west. He dismounted near the veranda.

Carson called to him. "Ned, what's going on out there in the west?"

"Stampede," replied McTammany laconically. "Couple of nesters been scarin' up steers."

"That's not so, Ned," declared Carson. "That dust has been moving for two hours and it's bunched. It's not a stampede, but the movement of a large, close bunch of steers."

"I've just come from that way," the foreman said steadily. "It's a stampede."

"You're lying!"

"All right, I'm lying. Which means I'm going." He turned back to his horse, mounted. He headed his horse back toward the west. But he rode only a few yards before wheeling his horse and riding back—eastward.

Helen, stepping off the veranda, saw the reason. Two horsemen were approaching from the west. A strange duo, consisting of Amos Holterman and Machamer, the biggest rancher in the valley after Major Carson. Major Carson half rose from his seat when he saw the new arrivals.

The horsemen dismounted and came toward the veranda. Machamer went into it without wasting time. "Carson, do you know that Nick Fedderson's moved out with his entire bunch and is stripping the range of steers? Did you know that?" His voice rose sharply, accusingly.

Major Carson's eyes flashed fire. "Damn you, Machamer, what are you saying?"

"I know that your foreman's in with Fedderson."

"I guessed that about two minutes ago. That was McTammany who rode away from here when you came up."

"Carson," Machamer said ominously. "I don't believe you."

"Call me a liar?" snarled Carson. "Why, damn you, Machamer, you come here with Holterman who's been fighting us all the time and you accuse *me* of being in cahoots with the wild bunch. Get off my place!"

"We're going," said Machamer, "but we're declaring ourselves right now. That bluff of them taking your stock along with ours don't go. Captain McNeilly's bringing in a company of Rangers and we're throwing in with them. Got that, Carson?"

"Helen," the major said grimly, "get my gun!"

"Uncle!" Helen cried. "And you men—listen. This has been as much of a surprise to us as it has to you. Uncle Raymond knew nothing about McTammany being in with the outlaws until a few minutes ago. You're making a mistake Mr. Holterman, my uncle believes——"

"He can believe what he likes," Amos Holterman retorted. "He's accused us farmers right along of doing things that we didn't do. He's said——"

"Skaggs!" roared Major Carson. "Bill Skaggs, come a-running!"

A bandy-legged cowboy popped out of the bunkhouse, came toward the main house as fast as his bowed legs could carry him. Other cowboys followed.

Machamer and Holterman backed away. "All right, Carson," Machamer said coldly, "if that's the way you want it . . ."

"I want it just like that!" snapped Major Carson. "My men start shooting in thirty seconds."

Machamer and Holterman mounted their horses, sent them away from the ranch house at a gallop. With an effort, Major Carson got up to his feet, favoring his wounded leg.

"Boys," he said to his cowboys, "Ned McTammany's sold us out to Nick Fedderson. They're cleaning the range of stock and it's my idea they're going to run the stuff across the river. We've got to go after them." He winced. "I mean, *you've* got to go after them."

18

Almost two hundred outlaws responded to Nick Fedderson's call. They came from all through the hills, two hundred men who had no homes, who hated law and order and everything that went with it.

Nick Fedderson spread out a crude map before a half dozen of the subchiefs whom he had appointed or who had declared themselves as more than rank and file.

"This," he said, pointing with a calloused finger, "is Broken Wagon Valley. The different ranches are marked here—Carson's, Machamer's, Welch's. I haven't marked the little places because there are too many of them. We can count on from ten to twelve thousand head from Carson's place alone. Take everything, but don't stop for cripples. We're going to be crowded and speed's the thing that'll win for us. McNeilly'll be here tomorrow, and I guess I don't have to tell you that he hasn't been *arresting* anyone lately."

He turned the map over to the others to study, and walked over to where Luke Vickers and Slater were waiting with a force of between forty and fifty men.

"The fightin's up to you. The rest won't have time; they've got to prod the herd along. Remember, it's a big game and a hard one. It's you boys who're holding the aces."

"Cut the speeches, Nick," snapped Vickers. "Let's get going!"

Fedderson swore in high humor. "You're fightin' mean,

Luke. That's fine. Just keep thinkin' of that gold you're going to have tomorrow and you'll come through all right. You, too, Slater."

They were off then, with Vickers and Slater riding at the head of the fighting force. They rode out of the hideout valley, over the rocky mountain trail into the big valley beyond. Fedderson's force followed but when they reached the big valley they broke up into smaller groups. Vicker's and Slater's group remained intact, however. The outlaws moved openly for their force was too large to conceal. The nesters dotted the valley, but they were isolated spots that could not offer much resistance.

Yet it was a nester who drew first blood. Riding in the wake of one of the roundup crews that swept along the farmer's two cows, the fighting force was fired upon. An outlaw took the bullet in the arm and cursing, immediately charged the farmer who took shelter behind a wagon. He fired a second time and the outlaw toppled from the saddle.

Vengeance was swift and spontaneous. A half dozen men broke from the main body, galloped down upon the wagon in a wide fan and riddled the farmer with revolver bullets. They were all for burning the man's house and barns, but Vickers, backed by Slater, prevented it.

"The smoke'll warn others," Slater advised.

It was an hour before sundown when Ned McTammany and Nick Fedderson came galloping out from a clump of cottonwoods.

"Head for the west two miles," Fedderson cried. "Carson's herd is over there and his men are heading for it. It's going to be a fight but we've got them beat two to one."

The troop wheeled to the left and went into a trot. McTammany fell in beside Slater. He leered wickedly. "Kinda surprised to see me in with the boys?" he asked.

"No," Slater said. "I guessed there was something crooked about you the first time I saw you."

McTammany snarled. "That's rough talk, for a man like you."

"Is it?"

"Yes, and I don't mind telling you that there's somethin' mighty fishy about you. You been askin' a lot of questions around here."

"About a man named Al Johnston? Ever hear of him?"

"I've known two-three Johnstons."

"This is a man who held up an express gold shipment in Colorado, about ten years ago, a man who's got ten thousand in gold that he's afraid to spend."

"Give me ten thousand in gold and I'll spend it, all right," McTammany said.

"This gold can be traced and Johnston knows it."

McTammany stared at him. "What are you—a detective?"

"I'm anything but that, I assure you."

"Then why should you be looking for a man who's got gold that can't be spent?"

"Because this man knows something about what happened to some people in Utah . . . at a place called Fort Starvation."

"Never heard of it."

"How long have you been with the Carsons?"

"Ever since they come out here, in '65."

"Then you've had plenty of chance to snoop through their things."

"Now look here, Slater, or whatever your name is, I've had just about enough from you . . ."

That was as far as he got, for the outlaw troop began pulling up. Fedderson and Vickers pulled up to Slater.

"There they are," said Fedderson, pointing.

The outlaws had stopped on a small rise. Down below was a grove of cottonwoods and in front of it were a number of cowboys, twenty or twenty-five. When the cowboys saw the outlaws on the ridge, they quickly retreated to the shelter of the cottonwoods.

"How should we fight them?" Fedderson cried. "They got the advantage of cover, so our two to one don't mean so much."

"We ought to split and have half our men take them from the rear or the side," Luke Vickers suggested.

Slater shook his head. "That might not work. While half our men are flanking them, the crowd down there might take a sudden notion to charge the rest of us. The odds would be even, but will our bunch stand up under a charge?"

Fedderson scowled. "Some will, some won't. They'll fight better if they got the edge."

"The answer's obvious then. Don't fight at all. The herd's out in the open. Why not just start prodding it along? Then

92

if the cattlemen want to fight they'll have to come after us—out in the open. And they'll have to do the attacking."

Fedderson exclaimed in satisfaction, "That's it, Slater. I'd just as soon not fight if I don't have to."

Slater knew that Fedderson would have to fight sooner or later, but he wanted to postpone the fight as long as possible —until the opposition became stronger and had a better chance of winning.

Fedderson communicated his orders to the troop of outlaws and with a wild yell they charged down upon the herd, stampeding it. It was a few moments before the cowboys in the cottonwoods divined the intent of the outlaws, and they then emerged from their concealment to find the outlaws, charging away from them. The cattlemen started in pursuit, but it became a rear-guard action, some of the outlaws hazing the cattle along, some carrying on a running fight with the pursuers. It was an inconclusive fight, but it gave Slater his opportunity.

In a wild charge of a dozen cattlemen, the outlaws scattered and Slater headed for a coulee. He distanced a couple of pursuers, climbed out and cut through a clump of cottonwoods. When he emerged from it, the firing was a mile or more distant. He was alone without another living soul within a mile.

19

Major Carson and Helen ate no supper that evening. The major tried limping along the veranda a little to ease the stiffness of his wounded leg, but he gave it up after a while.

"I wish those blasted Rangers had come," he exclaimed to his niece. "They'd ride roughshod over us, but at least we wouldn't be having this kind of thing."

"I can't understand why we haven't had any word from the men," Helen said. "They must know that we're anxious. You would think——"

She stopped, listening, then stepped off the veranda to the ground. "A horse—galloping!"

"At last!" cried the major.

The rider turned out to be John Slater. He dismounted in front of the house, came striding over to the veranda. Major Carson grabbed up a Colt from the chair in which he had been seated.

"You . . . !" he began.

"Hold it, Major," cried Slater. "I've got important information that may help you save your herd."

"I'll bet you have!"

Slater shifted quickly from the major to Helen. "Listen. I haven't got much time. You've got to believe me. Your men couldn't hold off Fedderson; there weren't enough of them. There aren't any single outfits large enough to fight. The other ranchers and the farmers are fighting little battles of their own and that's wrong, all wrong. You've got to unite, your own men and the others. And you've got to stop Fedderson where he can be stopped—in the hills. I've seen his maps and I know where he's headed. There's a place about fifteen miles from here, where he can be halted, maybe licked. But you can't do it without at least a hundred men."

"Slater," the major said ominously, "I advise you to clear out of here at once, before I shoot you down like the dog you are."

"Don't!" Slater exclaimed. "I don't give a damn for myself, but you—and all these men in Broken Wagon Valley are licked unless you get together and make a united effort."

The pounding of many horses' hoofs became suddenly distinct. Helen Carson cried out, "John, you'd better go!"

Her concern for him caused Slater to whirl on Helen. "Believe me, I'm telling the truth. Go to Holterman. He'll believe."

"You and Holterman," the major said thickly. "Damn you!"

"Uncle!" Helen said sharply. "He's telling the truth. Mary told me. He surrendered his gun to her father so he wouldn't have to kill Mr. Holterman. Mr. Holterman admitted it yesterday."

The approaching horsemen thundered into the ranch yard. Slater whipped out his gun, but a voice from the darkness roared:

"Hold everything! We're Rangers!"

Slater inhaled sharply. For him these new arrivals were as dangerous as Fedderson's outlaws.

Horses milled in the ranch yard, then two men walked into the shaft of light from the ranch house. One was Johnny Buff. The other was a tall, fierce-eyed man who wore a gun at each hip, butts turned forward.

"McNeilly," he said in a crackling voice as he came forward.

Major Carson exclaimed in a relief-flooded voice, "Thank the Lord!"

"Ha!" said Captain McNeilly. "I didn't expect to hear that from *you* from what I've heard about you, Major Carson."

"I didn't expect ever to say it," Major Carson replied fervently. "And I'll repeat it. Thank the Lord for the Texas Rangers. You got your company with you?"

"No," snapped McNeilly. "But they'll be here by morning. Right now I've got only twenty men with me. But I understand you have about thirty men. I want to swear them in——"

Carson groaned. "They're all out fighting Fedderson."

Johnny Buff raised himself on his toes and said something inaudible into his superior's ear. McNeilly whirled on Slater.

"You, Slater, what do you mean shooting up my best men?"

Slater made no reply. None was necessary. McNeilly glowered at him. "What are you doing here? Buff told me you'd gone into the hills."

"I came back," said Slater. "To tell Major Carson how to stop Fedderson."

"He's lying, Captain McNeilly," Major Carson snapped.

Captain McNeilly turned abruptly to Helen. "What do you think, Miss? Is Slater to be trusted?"

Without looking at her uncle, Helen said, "Yes."

McNeilly turned to Slater. "What's your plan?"

"Fedderson has his outfit split up into a half dozen units, with one strong fighting force that's supposed to range where it's needed. But the entire bunch will converge upon the trail leading through the hills. There's a pass, fifteen miles from here, where he can be stopped with a good force."

"But how are we going to get past him? He's already in the hills by now. He can beat us to the pass."

"No, he can't. He's got twenty thousand steers with him—he can't get to the pass before morning. You could cut across a couple of ridges and get there two hours sooner. Here . . ."

Slater stooped and with a finger drew several quick lines in the ground. "Here are the ridges, and here, winding through, is the trail Fedderson's got to take with the herd. He can't cut across the ridges with the cattle, but horses can and if you'll take your men here, you'll be at this place by sunup." Slater drew a short straight line. "You can stop Fedderson here with fifty men."

"I haven't got fifty men."

"My men are chasing Fedderson," the major said suddenly. "We can catch up with them and pull them off, then make the flank and cut across the ridges."

"That's what we'll do. Slater"—the Ranger Captain gripped Slater's shoulder—"I want you to go back with Fedderson."

"By now he knows I've deserted."
"It's up to you to convince him that you haven't."
"And if I do convince him, what then?"
"Draw your own conclusions."

20

The sun was just rising as John Slater studied the cabin-studded little valley that had been headquarters for Fedderson. It was empty of life now, but it wouldn't be for long.

A low rumble that shook the earth like a subterranean murmur told Slater thousands of cattle were approaching. The first he saw of them was a cloud of dust far up the narrow defile. After a few minutes the steers appeared, a long, narrow sea of them. There was only one direction for them to go, ahead, and they moved along quickly.

The outlaws brought up the rear.

Slater headed his horse down toward the biggest cabin in the little valley and standing close beside it, watched the bawling steers as they swirled past him.

He did not hear the step behind him, so when Alfred Orpington came up next to him he gave a tremendous start.

"Hello, Slater," Orpington said casually.

"What're you doing here?" Slater asked sharply.

"Why, you knew I was around here somewhere, didn't you? I thought Susan told you."

"She did. As a matter of fact, I've been expecting to run into you, but . . . well, not here."

"What's the matter with this place?"

Slater nodded toward the riders now approaching along the side of the herd. "You know who those men are?"

"Nick Fedderson's boys. And there's Nick." Orpington

chuckled. "Hold on, Slater. You're going to get the shock of your life."

"I'm beginning to suspect it already. You're the agent of the West Indies Government, who's buying this stolen stock."

"A man's got to make a living, doesn't he? So when I ran into this man down in New Orleans and learned he was in the market for cattle I saw no reason why I shouldn't cut myself in for a little profit. Nothing wrong with that, is there?"

"Not if the Texas Rangers don't catch you."

Orpington shrugged. "A bunch of Confederates."

"Here in Texas they're the law."

"Not west of the Pecos. Ah, here's Nick himself."

Fedderson, Vickers, McTammany and two or three other outlaws rode forward. Fedderson's eyes were on Slater.

"You damn traitor!" he grated as he came up.

"Traitor? Have Carson's men been dogging you since last night? Who do you think took them off your back?"

Fedderson's eyes narrowed. "You claim that *you* got rid of them?"

"I convinced them that the place to fight you was at the river, about twenty miles above where you're going to cross."

"He lies, Nick," cried McTammany. "Carson would have shot him down on sight."

"No, he wouldn't. He knows it was *you* started all the trouble between him and Holterman.

"You're a liar!" snarled McTammany.

"All right, McTammany, you've asked for it. You've got a gun . . ."

But a palsy suddenly shook McTammany.

"Well, McTammany, am I lying?"

"Go ahead, Ned," Vickers urged. "Put up or shut up."

McTammany still refused to accept Slater's challenge. Fedderson gave him a look of utter contempt and dismounted. He gestured to Colonel Orpington.

"There's a little matter we've got to settle, Colonel."

"Quite right. If you'll wait one moment . . ." Colonel Orpington smiled pleasantly, stepped back into the cabin and reappeared almost instantly with a small carpet valise. He dropped it on the ground in front of the cabin.

"Your down payment, Fedderson."

Fedderson started to reach for the bag, then suddenly straightened. "The agreement was gold."

Colonel Orpington indicated the bag. "Gold."

Fedderson stooped again, unfastened the sack. He reached in, stirred the contents, then brought out a fistful of gold double eagles. "There isn't a hundred thousand in this bag."

"Of course not," said the colonel pleasantly. "There's ten thousand."

"The agreement was a hundred thousand here and the balance on delivery across the river."

"Mr. Fedderson," Colonel Orpington said patiently, "I ask you—would a man bring a hundred thousand dollars here?"

"Why not?"

"Don't be ridiculous. Would a dog carry a pork chop into a den of hungry wolves? Your men are thieves, Fedderson, thieves and highwaymen. That ten thousand shows my good faith."

Luke Vickers's eyes blazed as he shot a look at Fedderson. "You said a hundred thousand here, Nick."

"So I did and a hundred thousand was the deal. We don't move this cattle until he coughs up the other ninety thousand."

Colonel Orpington shook his head. "You can't hold the cattle here, Fedderson. You know that as well as I do. You'll get the rest of the money on the other side of the river."

"I don't trust you worth a damn."

"Then we understand each other. I don't trust *you*, either. So shall we move along?"

The colonel stooped, prepared to close the carpetbag as soon as Fedderson dropped the handful of coins back into the bag. But Slater suddenly moved forward.

"Let me see that money!" he cried in a terrible voice.

Fedderson, shocked, let a couple of the coins slip from his fist. Slater scooped up one of the coins, took a quick glance at it.

"Where'd you get this money?" he demanded of Orpington.

"It's good money."

"This is a Clark and Gruber double eagle." He snatched another coin from Fedderson's hand. "And so is this."

"Those gold pieces are solid gold," said Colonel Orpington. "They're legal tender anywhere. If anything, they're worth

100

more than the government issue, which is made from a gold alloy."

"I know that," Slater said grimly. "But I still want to know where you got these coins?"

"Now Slater, I don't have to tell you that. The money's good and——"

Slater reached out, grabbed Colonel Orpington's collar and clutched it tight. "Where did you get it?"

In a fine rage, Orpington brushed off Slater's hand. "You're going too far."

"Don't you understand, Orpington?" Slater cried. "It was a coin like this that brought me here to Texas. The man who called himself Al Johnston gave one to Sergeant Lake in Arizona."

"What's that?" Orpington's eyes flickered to Ned McTammany. "Why, that would mean . . ."

Slater had already caught Orpington's look. He whirled, hit McTammany savagely in the face with the back of his hand. "So you're Al Johnston. He got the money from you."

"That's a lie," whimpered McTammany.

Orpington stepped up to McTammany. "The game's up, Johnston, if that's your real name. You knew Sergeant Lake."

"You can't prove it," whined McTammany. "You can't prove nothin'."

"I don't have to prove anything," Slater said savagely. "What were you trying to find out from Sergeant Lake? Answer me, or so help me . . ."

Nick Fedderson, who was standing by, jaws slack, suddenly moved forward. "Now, wait a minute, you fellows. What's this all about?"

"It's nothing that concerns you," Slater said.

"Everything around here concerns me," snarled the outlaw chief. "Where would a man like McTammany, or Johnston, or whatever you call him, get ten thousand in gold?"

"He held up an express shipment ten years ago," Slater said, "then he found out that he couldn't spend the money, because this was the total number of such solid gold coins that were made. It was as bad as if the coins were marked. They could be traced to him. He's been afraid to spend the money all these years."

"That right?" Orpington asked ominously.

"What's the difference?" McTammany snarled, suddenly bracing himself. "This money was going to Mexico——"

"It could still be traced to Mexico."

"But not to me!"

"No, not to you. You were going to take *my* money and skip with that, eh?"

"You think you're so smart?" sneered McTammany. "You and John Slater. You come down here snooping around, trying to find out what the Carsons knew. Well, I knew everything five years ago. I knew that the girl's father was eaten by a bunch of cannibals. I knew about the gold that was there in Utah. I knew about Lake and Bonniwell and I knew about you, Slater. You didn't fool me none, when you rode in here."

"What did you know about Bonniwell?"

"I know where he is."

"Where?"

"That's for me to know and you to find out."

Zing!

A rifle bullet whined over the heads of the outlaws. It was followed instantly by another, then a regular fusillade. The outlaws whirled, started forward toward the far end of the valley. Then they began milling their horses.

For down from the trail at the far end of the little valley, came a stream of riders. Fifty men . . . a hundred. Men armed with rifles, as well as revolvers. Texas Rangers.

"It's the Rangers!" roared Nick Fedderson. "They've cut us off!"

The Rangers began to fan out, riding past the cattle pouring forward. They came at a full gallop, firing. An outlaw went down from his horse, another.

Luke Vickers came toward Slater, his face distorted in savage fury. "You sold us out!" he cried.

His gun was already in his hand. Slater threw himself sidewards off his horse. Vicker's gun cracked and a bullet hit the dirt inches from Slater's head. Slater rolled over completely, came up to his knees, his gun in his hand.

The gun bucked and roared. Vickers's horse was suddenly riderless. A white-hot brand seared Slater's left shoulder. He half turned. Ned McTammany, on foot, blood streaming from a face wound, was rushing down on him.

Slater whipped up his gun. It roared at the same instant

102

that McTammany's gun spat flame and lead. McTammany fell forward on his face. Slater crawled to him as McTammany tried to lift himself up.

"Where's Bonniwell?" Slater cried.

"Damn you to hell!" McTammany choked. Blood gushed from his mouth. "Damn you to hell . . ." He fell forward again on his face, shuddered.

Slater grabbed the dying man's body, turned it over. A half smile parted McTammany's lips.

"Ask Bligh—ask Curtis Bligh—'bout Bonniwell . . ."

He lived another half minute, but those were the last words he uttered. When Slater rose to his feet, the fight in the valley was about over. Some Rangers were pursuing the remnants of the outlaw band, but McNeilly was riding back toward the group of cabins. Slater watched him approach.

McNeilly dismounted, came over.

"Who's that?" he asked, indicating McTammany's body.

"Major Carson's foreman. He sold out to Fedderson."

McNeilly scowled. "Can't trust anybody these days. I'll bet Fedderson was the first to run when the shooting started."

"No." Slater walked over a few feet, looked down at the dead face of Fedderson. "He didn't run at all. Here he is."

McNeilly came over, looked down at the dead outlaw chieftain. "All right, Slater, you did your job. You held them up long enough for us to come down on them. You can go."

The body of Colonel Orpington was not among the dead. He had made his escape.

21

Slater got out of the carriage before the Headquarters Building in Jefferson Barracks, near St. Louis. He said to the driver, "I may be a little while, but I'd like you to wait."

In the building an orderly directed him to the office of Lieutenant Colonel Peoples.

After the formalities were over, Colonel Peoples said, "Since receiving your letter I've been doing a lot of checking up on this matter." He shook his head. "Messy affair."

"My father was involved in it," Slater said.

"I know. And that's why I spent so much time on it." He pulled out a drawer, extracted a large Manila envelope and emptied the contents onto his desk.

"There were five men. Your father, John Slater, Douglas Carson, George Lake, Axel Turnboom and Stephen Bonniwell. The Army spent a considerable amount of time and effort trying to locate the next of kin. In the case of Axel Turnboom no next of kin was ever located." He glanced at one of the papers. "For that matter, his identity was established only by the initials found on one of the revolvers and a letter addressed to Axel Turnboom, by a dry goods store in Logansport, Indiana. It seems Turnboom had left Logansport owing a small bill of eight dollars and fifty cents. In Logansport our investigators learned that Turnboom was a bachelor, with no known kin. He'd been raised in the county orphanage and was employed as a sort of odd-job man around town until he went west in '57. . . ."

Slater nodded. "That checks with what I learned myself."

Colonel Peoples looked sharply at Slater. "You've been in touch with the next of kin of all these people?"

"All that I could locate, the brother of George Lake, a sergeant in the Fourth Cavalry, the daughter of Douglas Carson, who lives with her uncle in Texas."

"That leaves Bonniwell." The colonel consulted the sheet of paper again. "A brother, James Bonniwell, Ionia, Michigan."

"James Bonniwell enlisted in the Fourteenth Michigan Volunteers in July, 1861. He was wounded at Chickamauga, was invalided home, but never arrived in Michigan."

The colonel nodded. "Not an unusual case. He was afraid he might have to return to his regiment. We called them cowards."

"You've been on the plains lately, Colonel?" Slater asked.

"Just finished two years' duty at Fort Laramie, four months ago."

"And you never heard of Jim Bonniwell?"

The colonel looked at Slater, puzzled, then suddenly exclaimed, "Jim Bonniwell, the outlaw?"

"The same."

Colonel Peoples shook his head. "In Wyoming a lot of people think he's worse than Jesse James."

"Bonniwell's known," Slater said. "Why hasn't the law been able to get him?"

Colonel Peoples chuckled. "Apparently you're not familiar with western Wyoming where the Bonniwell gang holes up. Go out there some time."

"I intend to."

"To get Jim Bonniwell?" The colonel's eyes narrowed. He pursed up his lips thoughtfully, nodded slowly. His eyes flickered to the papers on his desk. He shifted them around, glancing at one sheet. Then he drew a deep breath.

"You had a quite a talk with Major Benjamin out in Fort Ogden, some time ago."

"That's right. There's no secret about any talk anyone has with the Army."

"In the Army there's always a higher-up. You know that yourself. You've got to have the answers when a higher-up

105

asks you the questions. You weren't satisfied with the report on the death of your father—a ten-year-old report. Odd, you waited ten years."

"I got the original report in '61 immediately after I'd enlisted in the Army. When I resigned my commission in '65 I returned to school to get my diploma——"

"That still gave you four or five years."

"Three," Slater said. "I left school in '67. Then I had to earn some money to enable me to make my search."

"Search for what? Foul play? The officer who made the original report said evidence of an Indian massacre was quite obvious. The—the other"—Colonel Peoples winced—"the other details are not pleasant, but they are not entirely without precedent. You've heard of the Donner Party in '47?"

"Of course. If it was only that . . ." Slater shrugged. "Lieutenant Orpington's report said that his detail buried five men. I have proof that six men were at Fort Starvation."

The colonel exclaimed, "Six!" His eyes darted to the papers.

Slater took out his wallet, extracted a faded, much creased letter. He opened it carefully, handed it to Colonel Peoples. The latter read it through and leaned back.

"It's a well-written letter . . ."

"My father was an educated man."

Colonel Peoples nodded. "He states that he is spending the winter with five companions and that he is mailing this letter from Salt Lake, while in the city to get supplies for the winter." The Colonel frowned, tapped the letter with a fingernail.

"This gold . . . no mention of it is made in Lieutenant Orpington's report." He looked up sharply. "Is that what's behind all this?"

"I believe so. When my father returned to Fort Starvation there were six men there, but only five were buried by Lieutenant Orpington. I want to find out what became of the sixth man."

"And the gold?"

"No," Slater said bluntly. "I don't care for the gold. I'd give it all right now if I could put my hand on the sixth man —the one who deserted the other five, perhaps helped the Indians to massacre them. I'd give the gold to Orpington right now."

"Orpington?"

"He's also trying to find the sixth man—so he can get the gold."

"This is Lieutenant Orpington you're talking about—the man who found the—remains of Fort Starvation?"

"Colonel Orpington—Brevet-Colonel Alfred Orpington. He resigned from the Army in 1865."

Peoples's fingers drummed his desk top. "Alf Orpington and I were classmates at West Point, although I haven't seen him since 1857. You're insinuating then that Orpington found this gold and appropriated it to his own use?"

"I'm not insinuating anything of the kind," Slater said bluntly. "In fact, I'm *sure* he didn't come upon the gold. My father's letter says that it was cached away for the winter somewhere *near* the Fort. Colonel Orpington could not have found the gold, not without his men being aware of it."

Colonel Peoples's face showed relief. "I'm sorry, Slater. While Orpington and I were not overly friendly at The Point, I still knew him quite well and to give him his due, I did not think he was the sort who would *steal*."

"What sort of people *do* steal, Colonel?" Slater asked sharply. "Born criminals? Or trusted servants of the public? Every man has his price. With some it's money, with others——"

"With some it might be revenge." Colonel Peoples suddenly evened up the edges of the sheets, slipped them back into the Manila envelope. "Is there anything else?"

Slater regarded Peoples steadily. "I want a copy of Colonel Orpington's service record."

Peoples exclaimed, "But you just said——"

"I said he didn't get the gold. But Orpington's been paralleling my own search. Everywhere I've gone, he's gone. He was in Arizona, in Colorado and then in Texas. He knows things that I don't know and I want to find him. I want to know every place he's served, every place he's lived. I want to back track, because I lost him in Texas and I want to find him."

"I don't know," said Colonel Peoples. "The Army doesn't like to give out information to civilians."

"I put in four years in the Army myself."

"Then you ought to know regulations." Peoples shook his head. "We may have to write to Washington."

"Washington will refer it to the Western Department. This is Headquarters for the Western Department."

"The request will have to be approved by the General."

"I served under General Sheridan."

Peoples brightened. "I'll make a note of that in my request." He got to his feet. "It'll have to go through channels. Leave your address and I'll mail you the report . . . if it's approved."

"My address is the Planters Hotel."

Colonel Peoples wrote it down. Slater shook hands with the colonel and left the building.

His carriage was waiting outside. Susan Orpington was sitting in it.

"You've been inside a long time," she said, as Slater opened the door.

"The colonel's with you?"

"I haven't seen him since—since Texas."

"But you knew *I'd* be here?"

"I asked myself what I'd do if I were you and learned certain things in Texas. I decided that if I were you and I ran into Colonel Orpington in Texas under—under suspicious circumstances, I decided that I'd come to Jefferson Barracks, which has all the records of all soldiers who ever served in the Western Department. I got here ten minutes after you did and the orderly told me that Colonel Peoples was engaged with a civilian named John Slater. So—well, here I am."

Slater climbed into the carriage and seated himself beside Susan. "The Planters Hotel," he told the driver. Then he turned to Susan. "Is that all right?"

"I'm staying there myself." She settled back against the cushion. "What happened to him, John? Captain McNeilly of the Rangers knew nothing about him and I—I looked over the bodies that were brought in to Broken Wagon."

"He got away."

"But why hasn't he written to me? It's not like Dad. Even if he didn't want to come and see me, he would have written. I waited a week and then I stopped off in Lawrence. There's been no word from him."

Slater shook his head. "You know him better than I do."

"You talked to him down there in the hills?"

"Yes."

"Did you learn anything of his plans?"

"I learned that he was planning to steal about a half million dollars, the proceeds from the sale of stolen cattle."

Susan winced at Slater's bluntness and was silent for a long time. They were entering the environs of St. Louis before she spoke again.

"Dad's failed at everything he's tried. He finished the war a brevet-colonel, when men his junior were generals. His permanent rank was only captain and a—a boy named Custer was made a lieutenant-colonel. He failed in business. He—he needs money."

"Some men get jobs," Slater reminded grimly.

"Some men can *hold* jobs. Dad can't. He needs money."

"All right," said Slater, "if he helps me find the sixth man he can have the gold, the entire sixty thousand. I don't want any of it."

Susan looked at him oddly. "What sixth man?"

"He hasn't told you? The sixth man who was at Fort Starvation."

"There were only five—your father, Douglas Carson, Axel Turnboom, George Lake and Stephen Bonniwell."

"There were six. Five died, but the sixth lived. I have reason to believe that he's alive today."

"I never knew." Susan frowned. "And that's why you're in this? You want to find this—this sixth man. Why?"

"Because I believe he betrayed the other five to the Indians."

Again Susan lapsed into silence. She did not speak again until they reached the Planters Hotel. Slater helped her out of the carriage, paid the driver. Then Susan said:

"So it's vengence with you." She shuddered a little. "I—I don't think I like you, John Slater."

She went into the hotel.

22

Curtis Bligh looked up from the sheaf of papers as Slater entered the private office of the most famous detective in the country.

"Sit down, Mr. Slater," Bligh said, gesturing to a plush-covered armchair.

Slater seated himself. Bligh sized him up a moment, grunted, then turned a page in the sheaf of papers before him. He read a few lines, shook his head, then looked up again at Slater.

"This is your dossier, Mr. Slater," the great detective said. "I've had it made up since you were in here the day before yesterday."

"I couldn't write that much about myself," Slater said evenly.

"Your war record is excellent," Bligh said. "I see you were at Antietam. My men did a rather good job of reconnaisance before that battle. I told McClellan it would be a hard battle."

"It was. We got licked."

"That's not the way it'll be in the history books. But you're quite right. It wasn't a victory, so it had to be a defeat." Bligh made a brushing gesture of dismissal. "You're a Harvard man, Mr. Slater."

"That's against me?"

"Frankly—yes. You want to become a cowboy detective."

"A detective—not a cowboy."

"Just a figure of speech. You want to go against a band of ruffians, train robbers, killers."

"I want to get Jim Bonniwell and I think I can do the job."

"I wonder. I've lost four men already to Bonniwell. I've been on his trail since '66 and I'm no nearer getting him now than I was at the start. Yes, I want to get him, I want Jim Bonniwell badly. But I don't want to lose another man to him."

"If I'm killed you won't hear any complaint from me," Slater said with heavy sarcasm. "And I've no relatives to sue you."

"That's in your favor. Do you have any idea of what you might be against, if you invaded Bonniwell's territory?"

"I intend to try to get into his band—join him and destroy him from the inside."

"That's what you said the other day, and frankly the idea appealed to me." Bligh cleared his throat. "It's what I might have done myself, fifteen, even ten, years ago. And I think, in the end it's the only way anyone will ever get Bonniwell. But a college man, joining a band of outlaws! I don't know."

"Mr. Bligh," Slater said slowly, "I'd rather have an organization like yours behind me, because I think you can help me, but whether you employ me or not, I'm going to get Jim Bonniwell. Alone . . . if I have to."

Bligh leaned back in his chair and studied Slater. "I think you mean that."

"I do."

23

The best way to describe Beaver Rapids is to say that it was a big town for its size. It consisted of two rows of false-fronted frame shacks, interspersed with log cabins and a canyon between them. The town boasted a nice log-cabin jail and was kept well filled by Bernie Cassidy, reputed to be the best peace officer west of Ogallala. He had killed eight men and wounded only two.

Slater, wearing patched levis, down-at-the-heel boots, a woolen shirt and a flat-crowned black stetson, swung down from the stagecoach and looked up and down the street. He saw the sign of the Placer Saloon a short distance away and started for it. He hitched up the cartridge belt from which was slung a worn holster that contained a Navy Colt.

The Placer Saloon turned out to be a long, narrow room with a bar running down one side of it. A number of tables were scattered about and at the far end of the room was a low platform on which stood a weathered piano.

There were perhaps a dozen patrons in the place when Slater entered and moved to the bar. A stocky bartender ambled over.

"Whisky," Slater said harshly, "and I mean whisky, not the watered-down bilge you sell the local citizens."

The bartender got a bottle and a glass and set them down before Slater. "Pretty salty, aren't you?"

112

"Salty enough." Slater poured whisky to the very brim of the glass. As he picked it up, some of the stuff sloshed over onto the bar.

The bartender noted that and scowled. "From Texas, eh?"

Slater tossed down the whisky in a single gulp, shuddered and wiped his mouth with the back of his hand. "Any law against a man being from Texas?"

The bartender shrugged. "For all of me you could be from Jackson's Hole. But we got a marshal here who don't like Texas men. He don't like 'em a lot."

"Well, I don't like marshals. That makes us even."

He poured out another glass of whisky, again spilling a few drops. He set the bottle down and started to pick up the little glass. At that moment a youth of nineteen or twenty came through the batwing doors and strode up to the bar beside Slater.

He was a skinny kid wearing filthy levis and a floppy Stetson, but two gun holsters were tied low on his thighs. He gestured to the bottle in front of Slater.

"Gimme that."

Slater drank his whisky, gave the youth beside him a calm glance and, deliberately picking up the bottle, began to pour himself a third drink.

The kid's face distorted in sudden rage. "I said gimme that bottle."

Slater continued pouring out whisky slowly, carefully. "You ain't hardly old enough to drink," he said.

The bartender winced and held out a placating hand, not to Slater, but to the wild-eyed youth beside him.

"Now, wait a minute, kid!"

The boy ignored him. He stepped sideward, went into a crouch. "Look here, you moth-eaten saddle bum," he snarled at Slater, "do you know who I am?"

"A brat who isn't dry behind the ears!"

The bartender shouted. "He's Johnny Cool."

"Oh, yeah?" sneered Slater. Then he reached out suddenly and smacked Johnny Cool in the face with the back of his hand. The blow sent the boy reeling back, into the arms of a tall, well-built man in his mid-thirties, who had come up from behind.

Johnny Cool recoiled off the other man, started to reach for his guns. But the man with whom he had collided sprang forward and throwing both arms about the kid, pinioned them to his sides.

Johnny Cool struggled furiously in the man's grip. "Lemme go," he howled, "lemme go and I'll kill 'm. Nobody can slap Johnny Cool and live."

"Let him go, Mister," Slater said sardonically, "and I'll really slap down his ears for him. It's what he needs."

The man who was holding Cool whispered something into his ear and the youth eased off on his struggles. After a moment, the man released Johnny Cool. There was still fire in his eyes, however.

"All right," he said thickly to Slater, "all right this time, but the next time I see you, you better be wearin' your iron."

"What for?" Slater asked mockingly.

" 'Cause I'm tellin' you!" snarled Cool.

He lurched past Slater and headed for the door. Slater did not look after him. The man who had held Cool smiled quizzically at Slater, but there was no humor in the smile.

"Stranger," he said, "I got a hunch you aren't going to live to wear a long, gray beard."

"I'm doing all right."

"Sure, you're doing fine."

The other man shook his head and followed Cool through the door. Slater turned to the bar, picked up the bottle. The bartender let out a long, slow sigh.

"Mister," he declared fervently, "that's the closest you'll ever come to shovin' off without really makin' it."

Slater looked at the bartender in surprise. "A kid like that?"

"Ain't you never heard of Johnny Cool?" the bartender asked incredulously.

"Can't say that I have. Is he supposed to be bad?"

"Ain't none worse. Some say he's kill crazy. Lucky for you Mr. Parker grabbed him."

"*Mister* Parker?"

"Yeah, Alan Parker. He's got a big ranch up north a ways."

"Oh," said Slater, and poured out a glass of whisky.

He was still pouring out whisky two hours later. The lamps had been lit in the saloon by then and the place was crowded with evening patrons. Slater didn't see them, however. He could scarcely see the bartender.

He waved the empty whisky bottle in the direction he guessed the bartender would be.

"Gimme 'nother bottle this stuff you call whisky."

A voice from behind the bar said, "Don't you think you've had enough?"

No drunk has ever had enough, and the bartender should have known it. Slater banged the bar with his fist. "What's that, you jumpin' sidewinder? You tryin' to tell *me* how much I can drink? Why, you . . ."

He threw the empty bottle. The bartender dodged and the bottle hit the back mirror. The crash of the glass must have penetrated Slater's dull senses, for he backed away from the bar . . . into a table. He fell over the table, knocking it to the floor and scattering money and cards.

A card player swore feelingly, "You drunken bum!"

Slater rolled clear of the wreckage, got to his hands and knees. The card player kicked at him, but Slater lurched sideward and the foot missed him. He grabbed at it with both hands, upset the body behind the foot, then used it to climb to his feet.

He put up his hands, ready to take on all comers.

"All right, fellas," he challenged, "come ahead. One at a time, or all of you. It don't matter to me. I can lick any man in this damn town."

The marshal came swinging through the doors, heard the last of Slater's challenge. He was a lean, hungry-looking man with a black patch over his left eye socket. A wrongdoer had emptied that socket and Bernie Cassidy had a justifiable hatred for all wrongdoers.

He came up behind Slater. "All right, you." He grabbed Slater's left arm. Slater pivoted and his fist connected with Bernie Cassidy's jaw.

Bernie Cassidy reeled back. A glint came into his one eye. He whipped out his long-barreled Frontier Model. "You asked for this." he said tonelessly, then sprang forward and laid the barrel of the gun along the side of Slater's head.

24

A thousand little devils were pounding the side of Slater's head. The pain was exquisite but for a long time Slater could not fight it. Then suddenly he sat up and opened his eyes. The little devils disappeared, leaving just one great ache in his head.

The first glance around told Slater that he was in jail. His second look revealed a disreputable-looking oldster in the adjoining cell. The oldster was sitting on his cot, his back against the wall, studying Slater with morbid interest.

"How you feel?"

"Lousy." Slater touched the side of his face. "How'd I get here?"

The man in the adjoining cell showed blackened teeth in a grin. "Bernie Cassidy drug you in."

"Cassidy?"

"The marshal. He buffaloed you."

Slater winced. "I must have been drunk."

"Wouldn't be surprised. Sober now?"

"How long've I been here?"

"Oh, you came in early. Round seven. It's close to eleven now. Which is pretty quick soberin'—if you're sober."

"I'm sober."

The other man chuckled. "They call me Fresno."

"My name's Slater, John Slater."

"Howdy, Slater." Fresno chuckled again. "Didn't take you

116

long to get in here, did it? You on'y hit town this afternoon."

Slater scowled. "What're *you* crowing about? You're not exactly in church, you know."

"I'm in here by mistake." Fresno got up and came to the bars separating his cell from Slater's. "I got into an argument with the marshal. That was a mistake."

"This marshal's a tough character?"

"Bernie Cassidy? Ain't none tougher. But I got nothin' to worry about. Alan Parker'll get me out."

"I've been hearing of this Parker. He's a big man around here?"

"He's on'y the most important man in the territory," Fresno said enthusiastically. "Besides which, he's my boss."

"Does he pay you extra for the advertising?" Slater asked sarcastically.

"He don't have to," retorted Fresno warmly. "And lemme tell you somethin'——"

"Later. Just now I want to get out of here." Slater got up and went to the cell door. He gripped the bars and yelled at the top of his voice.

"Marshal! Marshal Cassidy!"

Fresno watched Slater with a jaundiced eye. "Go ahead'n yell. See if it'll do you any good."

Slater yelled again. A third time.

The door leading to the front of the building opened and Bernie Cassidy appeared. He looked dispassionately at Slater. "Now, look, you're not going to give me trouble tonight, are you? I was up all last night with a couple of drunks."

"I want to have a talk with you," Slater said.

"It'll wait until morning."

"It won't. I've got to get going."

"You can get along in the morning—after you pay your fine."

Slater lowered his voice. "I want to tell you something—about Chicago."

"Chicago?"

"Yes, Chicago."

Cassidy came up to Slater's cell and unlocked the door. Slater stepped out. Cassidy dropped his hand to the butt of his Frontier Model. "In my office."

Slater walked through the door. Cassidy followed.

Cassidy's office contained a rolltop desk, a couple of chairs,

117

a cot and reward notices and posters in lieu of wallpaper. Cassidy closed the door leading to the jail section.

"All right, now what's this about Chicago?"

"Ever been there?"

"Yes."

"Talk to a man about Vicksburg?"

Cassidy regarded Slater steadily. "Seems to me I did," he said evenly. "But I can't remember the man's name."

"Was it Bligh?"

"You sure picked a funny way to introduce yourself!" Slater touched his aching head. "I hadn't counted on the clout on the head."

"You're lucky that's all it was." Cassidy suddenly looked at the jail door. "I *would* have him here tonight."

"The old coot?"

"Fresno."

"He's one of them?"

Cassidy shrugged. "He hangs around with Johnny Cool sometimes." He suddenly pointed at Slater. "Heard you had a run-in with Johnny. What were you trying to do—commit suicide?"

"I didn't know who he was at the time." Slater frowned. "You think Cool's one of Bonniwell's boys?"

"Of him I'm sure. And I wouldn't be a bit surprised if old Fresno . . ." He shook his head. "That was bad—picking a fight with Johnny Cool. He may cause you trouble."

"Ornery, is he?"

"Don't know if he's the worst, or Billy Burks."

"Johnny Cool—Fresno—Burks. Who else do you suspect? What about Bonniwell?"

"Who's Bonniwell? A name. He could be anyone. If I knew who Bonniwell was Curtis Bligh wouldn't have had to send you here. By the way, what's your plan?"

"To get in with the gang."

Cassidy winced. "Are you serious? You couldn't get within twenty miles of Bonniwell's hideout."

"I'm going to try." Slater looked thoughtfully at Cassidy for a moment. "Look, Bonniwell's outfit is tough. We know that. They've been getting away with it for years. They're no longer local bad men. They're big time, so big that the railroads have hired Curtis Bligh—the greatest detective in the country."

"Sold on him, are you?" Cassidy asked.

"He's paying me my wages."

Cassidy nodded. "Look, Slater, I'm going to tell you a few things about Jim Bonniwell. I thought Bligh knew already."

"You mean about the ranchers being friendly to Bonniwell? About the gang's secret post offices up and down the Wasatch Range? The spies . . . ?"

Cassidy seated himself in the swivel chair before the rolltop desk. "You knew all that and you still think you can get in with Bonniwell?"

"Bligh thought you might be able to help."

"There's only so much I can do." Cassidy shook his head. "I don't know much about you, but the fact that Bligh picked you for this job means you're probably a pretty good man."

"I am," Slater said quietly.

Cassidy grunted. "You're going to have to be an awfully good man. Well, it's your funeral."

"Maybe it will be."

"There's a ranch about thirty miles from here—northwest. It's just on the edge. Run by a fellow named Kellerman. I'm thinkin' he might know the bunch. If he doesn't . . ." Cassidy shrugged. "You'll just have to keep going, north and west."

Slater moved to the desk, reached for the ring of keys Cassidy had put down. Cassidy exclaimed, "What's the idea?"

"I'm going to lock you up."

"No, you're not," Cassidy retorted grimly. "I'm willing to help you, but this is my town and——" He started to reach for his gun. He never touched it, for Slater hit him a hard blow that caught the mean marshal on the point of the jaw and sent him down cold.

Slater dragged him into the jail section, where Fresno watched with bulging eyes.

"Coming up, one marshal!" Slater sang out.

"Jumpin' Judas!" Fresno said in awe. "I don't believe it. Nobody could do that to Bernie Cassidy. Nobody."

"You can tell your grandchildren about it."

"If I had any grandchildren, which I ain't."

Slater deposited the unconscious marshal on the bunk that he had himself only recently vacated. Then he came out and locked the door. He looked at Fresno.

"Coming along?"

"You mean you're going to run for it?"

"That's the general idea."

Slater unlocked Fresno's cell, then tossed the keys through the bars into Cassidy's cell. Fresno scratched his head.

"I dunno, Cassidy ain't going to like this."

"Stay then. Explain to Cassidy that you weren't in on it. Think he'll believe you?"

Fresno hesitated, then came out of the cell. "You got a point." But there was a frown on his face. "Say, that talk between you and Cassidy, that Chicago stuff—what was that?"

Slater grinned. "I saw a poster down at the stage office. Five hundred dollars' reward for a Chicago bad man. Guess he thought I was him. That's when I hit him, while he was going through the reward notices."

Slater went through the door into the marshal's office. Fresno followed, but without much enthusiasm. Outside the jail building he became quite nervous.

A horse was tied to the hitchrail. Slater moved toward it. Fresno bleated, "That's Cassidy's horse!"

"Looks like a good animal."

"Are you crazy? You can't take Cassidy's horse."

"Why not? He can't do any more to me for taking his horse than for what I've already done to him."

"But everybody in sixty-six miles knows Cassidy's horse. I wouldn't be seen riding it for all the money in Wyoming."

Slater moved back reluctantly. "You may be right."

"Doggone right I am. You can get a horse at the livery stable. I got one there myself."

The livery stable was lighted by a single lantern under which the livery man sat in an armchair, sound asleep. Fresno kicked the chair and the liveryman came to his feet before his eyes were opened.

"Fresno! I thought you were in jail."

"I was."

"Cassidy let you go before morning? He must be getting soft."

"Maybe he is." Fresno gestured to Slater. "Can you fix up my friend with a good horse?"

"I want to buy one," Slater said.

The liveryman brightened. "I got just what you want, a

black gelding only five years old." He moved to a stall, opened it and brought out a black horse.

"Here he is, Mister. Yours for only a hundred and ten——"

"Sixty dollars!"

"I paid ninety-five for him." The liveryman was indignant.

"What'd you get with him? A gold-studded saddle and diamond bit? I'll give you seventy-five."

"Give him eighty," interposed Fresno, "if he throws in a saddle."

He chuckled and stepped into a stall. He came out leading a fine chestnut mare. He mounted and half saluted Slater.

"So long, pardner!"

"Wait a minute," Slater exclaimed.

"Can't. I'm in a hurry."

He dug his knees into the belly of the mare and the animal dashed out of the livery stable. Slater turned impatiently back to the liveryman.

25

Morning found Slater nearing the foothills. It was shortly afterwards that he encountered a farm wagon loaded high with furniture and farming implements. A man and a woman sat on the wagon seat. The man regarded Slater sourly as the latter pulled up, facing him.

"Howdy?" Slater said cheerfully.

"Howdy," was the curt reply.

"I'm a stranger hereabouts," Slater went on, "and I'm wondering if I've lost my way."

"Where're you headed for?"

"Kellerman's place."

The man on the wagon winced. "You're headed right, only you want to turn left when you get to the top of the next hill." He picked up his lines. "Good day to you."

"Good day," Slater said.

He rode on, reached the crest of the first hill and turned left. He entered a valley of wild beauty and after a while came to a little stream where he dismounted and hobbled his horse so that it could graze. He stretched out on the grass himself and was asleep in three minutes.

The sun was past the halfway mark when he awoke. He tightened his belt, caught the black gelding and mounted it.

It was late afternoon when he reached the crest of a low hill and looked down upon the Kellerman's place. It consisted simply of a log cabin, a log barn and a pole corral.

Slater rode up to the barn.

"Hello, there!" he called out cheerily.

Colonel Orpington came out of the barn. He wore levis, a flannel shirt and a flat-crowned, weathered Stetson.

"What kept you so long, Slater?" he asked.

Slater stared at Orpington, as grudging admiration welled up in him.

Susan Orpington came out of the house. She wore a gingham dress, her face was scrubbed, her hair twisted in a tight coil on the back of her head.

"Hello, John," she said easily.

Slater exhaled wearily. "Hello," he said and dismounted from his gelding. "I was under the impression that a man named Kellerman owned this ranch."

Orpington smiled thinly. "Kellerman was an old broken-down cattle rustler, who'd lived about twenty years longer than he'd had any right to. I bought this place from him. The whole shebang . . . three hundred dollars."

"I never thought of you as a farmer," Slater said slowly. He looked at Susan. "And I somehow can't figure you as a farmer's daughter."

"As a matter of fact," Susan said carefully, "I happen to like farming. We've got a couple of cows, some horses and chickens. And if you're staying for supper, you'll discover that I'm a rather good cook. I've got biscuits in the oven right now."

"You're staying?" Colonel Orpington asked.

"You couldn't drive me off." He regarded Susan steadily. "And I like biscuits, hot, with homemade butter."

The supper consisted of steak, potatoes and biscuits. When he was through eating, Slater said to Susan, "It's been a long time since I ate a meal as good as this."

"The food is very good at the territorial penitentiary," Susan said, "At least that's what some of our guests have told us . . . the guests we've had this past month."

"Jim Bonniwell's men?" Slater asked.

Orpington shrugged. "They don't trust me—yet. They think I'm a spy. But they stop here and eat, then go over the hill to the west." He paused. "For all I know, Bonniwell may have stopped here. These men don't give their names. And by the way, *our* name is Hastings."

Slater pushed back his chair, started to get up. Then sud-

123

denly he stiffened. From outside came the clop-clop of a horse's hoofs. Susan got up from the table, stepped past Slater to the door.

"It's Alan Parker," she said.

Orpington whirled on Slater. "What's your name?"

"Slater."

Orpington nodded, stepped to the door. "Come on in, Alan!" he called.

Alan Parker came into the house.

"Alan," Orpington said, "shake hands with John Slater."

Parker looked sharply at Slater. "Looks like I run into you everywhere I go." He took Slater's hand.

Slater grinned. "I owe you one for that business in the saloon. I heard about the kid later."

"I heard about *you* later." Parker shook his head. "Bernie Cassidy sends his regards."

Susan interrupted. "Alan, there's some steak left."

Parker rubbed his hands together. "Good."

Susan looked at Slater. "Stop in again, sometime, Mr. Slater, is it? When you're not in such a hurry."

"Thanks," said Slater. He went to the door. Orpington frowned slightly. He wanted to talk some more, but the presence of Parker interfered. He nodded.

Darkness fell within the hour, but Slater was well along the trail over the mountain by then. The country got rougher, but the trail was a well-defined one and the gelding followed it without difficulty. He was a sure-footed animal and the darkness did not seem to bother him. And after a while the moon came up.

After three hours of riding, Slater halted for a couple of hours, but did not go to sleep. When he climbed into the saddle again the gelding began to climb.

The trail became narrower and in a little while was no more than a shelf spiraling up a steep mountain. The gelding picked his way carefully, stopping once or twice.

The false dawn was graying the sky when the animal stopped again. Slater dismounted and worked his way carefully along the narrow ledge to the horse's head.

"Sorry," he said, and gave the reins a sharp jerk.

The gelding whickered and tried to retain his balance on the ledge, but lost it and slipped over the side. It scrambled

124

and slid to a ledge twenty feet below, where it regained its balance. Slater followed down, patting the horse.

Then he groped about the ledge and found a chunk of rock. He held it for a moment in his hand, then gritting his teeth, jammed it sharply against his knee.

He could not quite restrain a yelp of pain, and hopped up and down on one foot for a moment. Then the pain subsiding, he pulled up the trouser leg and exposed a nasty cut. He bound a bandana tightly about his knee, put down the trouser leg and remounted the gelding.

Dawn came grudgingly a half hour later and melted into daylight when Slater rode down into a flat, narrow valley that ended three or four miles away against a sheer cliff.

A little stream wound through the narrow valley. Slater rode beside it. Halfway down the valley he made out a rough shack, set almost against the cliff. The color of it had faded so that it seemed part of the cliff itself.

The end of the trail.

A bullet whined over Slater's head. Before the report of the rifle came, Slater was down on the ground, diving for the shelter of a large boulder beside the little creek.

The Frontier Model he had appropriated from Bernie Cassidy was in his hand as he peered carefully from behind the boulder.

Spang!

A bullet chipped a splinter off the boulder. Slater whirled, turned back as a bullet from the front kicked up sand near by. Then he got to his feet, his hands going slowly up to his shoulders.

A man stepped out from behind some boulders in front. In the rear a man with a rifle stepped out from a clump of scrawny cottonwoods.

"Drop the gun." the second man called.

Slater let the Frontier Model clatter to the ground. He looked toward the cabin, saw two men come running out. These he recognized: Old Fresno and Johnny Cool.

The two men who covered Slater awaited the approach of their reinforcements. It was Johnny Cool who first recognized Slater.

"The Beaver Rapids bad man!" he yelled.

Fresno looked unhappy. "How'd you come to follow me?"

"I didn't." Slater looked at Johnny Cool. "Hi, kid, how've you been?"

"I been wishin' I'd see you again," Johnny Cool said. He came forward, a cruel light in his eyes.

The man with the rifle moved forward swiftly. "Now, wait a minute, Johnny."

Fresno said hastily, "This is the fella I was tellin' you about —the man who got the drop on Bernie Cassidy."

Cool said icily, "I don't give a good goddam about Bernie Cassidy. But I owe this ranny somethin' and here's where I pay off."

The rifleman stepped in Cool's way. He dropped his gun.

Slater laughed without humor. "Oh, the boy wants gunplay, does he?" He started to stoop for the Frontier Model, but Fresno gestured him back with his own gun.

Slater said, "Well, if you shoot men out here without giving them a chance . . ."

"You'll get your chance," the rifleman said.

"Get out of the way, Rodebaugh," Johnny Cool snarled.

Fresno scooped up Slater's gun, looked at Rodebaugh. The latter moved sideward as Johnny Cool tried to step past him.

"Let him have his gun," Cool whined. "Let him have it. He took a crack at me in Beaver Rapids and I warned him to be wearin' his iron the next time I saw him."

"Well, let me have it," Slater said impatiently.

Rodebaugh shook his head stubbornly. "You'll touch no gun until the boss talks to you. And you, Johnny, you hold off. You know what the boss told us to expect."

The kid blinked, pointed at Slater. "Him?"

Rodebaugh nodded. "Yes."

Johnny Cool relaxed. "All right, I'll wait. But Jim's got to let me have him."

"He probably will," Rodebaugh said. He turned to Slater. "Come along, Mister."

Slater limped forward. "This Jim, suppose he might give me a job?"

"A job?" Rodebaugh asked sharply.

"This *is* a ranch, isn't it?"

Johnny Cool laughed wickedly. "Yeah, it's a ranch. Jim Bonniwell's ranch."

Slater looked at Fresno. "Thought you worked for Alan Parker?"

"I do, sometimes," Fresno replied.

Slater limped toward his horse. Fresno watched him. "Hurt your leg?"

"My horse fell." Slater pulled up his trouser leg, revealing a badly swollen thigh—from the too tight bandage. Fresno exclaimed in sympathy.

"Say, that looks bad."

"I've known it to feel better."

Slater seated himself on the ground, began to untie the bandana. Johnny Cool came up with the fourth outlaw.

"Mr. Hackett," he said mockingly, "like you to meet my friend, Mr. uh, Mr. uh . . . what'd you say your name was? Or don't detectives have names?"

Slater looked at him coolly. "Detective?"

"How's Mr. Bligh?"

Slater grinned. "Have your fun. This one's on me." He jerked the bandage off his wounded leg. Fresno dropped to one knee beside him.

"Here, lemme help you with that."

"Why bother?" Cool sneered. "Come noon and it won't hurt no more. None at all."

Rodebaugh moved up, took one look at Slater's knee and gestured to Fresno. "Get some water."

Fresno scrambled up and hurried to the stream. Taking off his hat, he filled it with water.

There was a chance, Slater thought. Fresno and Rodebaugh. Johnny Cool was against him and the fourth man, Hackett, seemed neutral. Put him on Cool's side. That would make it two and two. But Jim Bonniwell, the leader, would make the decision.

26

They were gathered outside the cabin toward noon when a rider appeared down the valley. Hackett and Johnny Cool went out to meet him, leaving Rodebaugh and Fresno to watch Slater.

Slater watched the approach of the newcomer with interest. He seemed strangely familiar, but it wasn't until he was within a hundred yards that he finally recognized him. It was Alan Parker.

"Jim Bonniwell, eh?" Slater said when Parker rode up.

"Jim Bonniwell. Bonniwell or Parker, take your choice." Bonniwell smiled. "Didn't think we'd meet again, did you?"

"No, I didn't."

Rodebaugh seemed puzzled. "Know him, chief?"

"I think so, Fred." The grin left the outlaw's face. "All right, Slater, you can drop it now."

"So you think I'm a detective, too?"

"Prove that you aren't."

"You prove I am."

"You mean the business in Beaver Rapids?" Bonniwell shook his head. "Doesn't mean a thing. You landed in town looking for a fight. You picked one with Johnny Cool, then with somebody else. You got thrown in the clink."

"He buffaloed Bernie Cassidy," Fresno offered.

"Maybe."

"Naw, Jim. I looked at Bernie and he was sure 'nough out —cold!"

"Bernie's a law man. It could have been a put-up job."

"You think so?" Slater asked carelessly.

"How come you headed right for Kellerman's place?"

Slater laughed. "You think this hideout is a secret? I heard about it in Cheyenne—in Ogallala. The Wild Bunch is known all over the west."

"But you hadn't heard about Johnny Cool."

"Oh, yes. I had."

Bonniwell glowered. "All right, maybe you weren't afraid of Johnny Cool."

"He'd better be afraid," howled Johnny Cool.

Bonniwell gestured him to silence. "You may be on the level, Slater."

"Thanks," said Slater mockingly.

Bonniwell looked at Slater through slitted eyes. "You've done a good job, Slater. I'll admit I'm not sure about Cassidy, but the Hastings say you acted like a man on the dodge, and you certainly traveled like a man in a hurry." His eyes dropped to Slater's leg. "What's the matter with your leg?"

"Pretty bad bruise." Rodebaugh said. "I looked at it."

"Where'd it happen?"

"On the other side of the mountain," Slater said, pointing. "Up near the top, where the trail gets narrow. My horse slipped to a ledge below."

Bonniwell's eyes glowed. "Fred," he said to Rodebaugh, "take a trip up the trail. Check on that."

Rodebaugh nodded and went for his horse.

Bonniwell looked steadily at Slater. "Nobody but a damn fool—or a man in a hurry would travel most of the night. If your story checks, Slater . . ." He shrugged.

27

Rodebaugh came into the cabin in the late afternoon. He nodded in response to Bonniwell's inquiring look. "Horse fell, all right. And there was a stone with some blood on it."

"So I pass," Slater said laconically.

Johnny Cool, who had been held in restraint all day by Bonniwell, advanced on Slater. "Not with me you don't pass," he snarled.

"All right, sonny," Slater said calmly, "You've been asking for it."

He walked toward the rough table where his Frontier Model lay. But Bonniwell covered the gun with his hand. "Wait a minute, you two."

"I'll fill him full of holes," Cool promised.

"You won't do anything of the kind," Bonniwell declared emphatically. "I'll have no shooting in this outfit. I've warned you about that time and again, Johnny.

"He hit me," the boy whined.

"I'll hit you again if you don't keep your mouth shut," Slater warned.

"Cut it, Slater," Bonniwell snapped.

"Sure," said Slater and, taking a quick step forward, slapped Johnny Cool in the face.

Johnny screamed and reached for his gun. Before he got it, Slater snatched his own gun from under Bonniwell's yielding hand, threw it on Johnny. The boy's hand stopped on the butt of his gun—still in its holster.

"You didn't beat me fair," he howled. "Nobody can beat me on the draw. Nobody."

Bonniwell stepped between Johnny Cool and Slater. He knocked down Slater's gun and placed the flat of his other hand on Johnny Cool's chest.

"One more stunt like this and you're through in this outfit," he said ominously. "The both of you."

"I don't take lip from any squirt who ain't dry behind the ears," Slater said through bared teeth.

"You'll take orders from me," the outlaw chieftain ordered. "And this is an order."

Slater relaxed and dropped his Frontier Model into his waiting holster. "All right, Bonniwell."

Johnny Cool was still slobbering but he backed away. Bonniwell faced both of them. "I guess there's too much tension in this crowd. What we need is some fun."

"Ocelot Springs, Jim?" Rodebaugh asked eagerly.

Bonniwell nodded. "This is Saturday."

Ocelot Springs was a tiny hamlet of perhaps twenty buildings. It was located in a narrow valley, a dozen miles from the hideout, deep in outlaw territory. It was too small a place to boast a marshal.

It was still daylight when the outlaws rode up the dusty street and tied their mounts in the front of the only saloon in Ocelot Springs.

Johnny Cool was the first one in the saloon. He was followed by Hackett and Fresno. Bonniwell tied his mount leisurely, then rubbed his chin with the back of his hand.

"Guess I'll get a shave," he said to Slater.

Slater nodded. "I want to buy a couple of things in the store. Suppose I meet you here in a half hour."

"I'd rather you picked me up at the barbershop," Bonniwell said meaningly.

"I get it," Slater chuckled. "Don't want me alone with Johnny."

"That's the general idea."

He entered the little barbershop. Slater saw him sit down in the single chair, then walked up the street to the general store, a rather large one for such a small community.

131

In the rear of the store was a counter and a wicket over which was a sign: U.S. POST OFFICE.

The store was vacant of customers, and the proprietor, a middle-aged Swede, came forward.

"Howdo, stranger."

"Like to get some tobacco," Slater said. "And a box of .45 cartridges."

"Sure t'ing."

The storekeeper got the tobacco and cartridges, and Slater paid for them. He started to turn away, then glanced at the "Post Office."

"Can you sell me a sheet of paper and an envelope and maybe a stamp?"

The storekeeper got the items. Slater borrowed a pencil and scrawled a note. He was addressing the envelope when a door in the rear opened and Jim Bonniwell entered. He bore down swiftly on Slater.

Slater folded his letter and inserted it in an envelope. Then he saw Bonniwell.

"You didn't get your shave."

Bonniwell held out his hand. "Let me see that letter."

Slater hesitated. "It's just a note to my uncle in Texas." He handed the letter to Bonniwell.

The outlaw chief glanced at the envelope and seemed surprised. "Mordecai Slater," he read. "Sherman, Texas." He took out the letter, skimmed through it. His forehead creased in thought. He read the letter a second time.

"So you're wanted in Texas!"

"I don't know for sure. There was a little trouble, but . . ." Slater grinned. "I'm staying away for a while, just in case."

Bonniwell nodded. "And this Angela?"

"A neighbor. There wasn't anything between us."

"But you send your love."

"Just a way of talking."

Bonniwell refolded the letter, sealed it and dropped it in the mail chute.

"Pretty careful, aren't you?" Slater couldn't help saying.

"That's why I'm still in business," Bonniwell retorted. Then suddenly he grinned. "Now let's get shaved and go to the dance."

"Dance? Here?"

"And how!"

The shaves took an hour, by which time Slater and Bonniwell could already hear the strains of music up the street. When they got to the hall where the dance was being held it was quite dark and the dance was in full progress.

The room was small, but crowded. A lot of people seemed to live in the hills, although you could travel through them for days and see only an isolated farmhouse or two. But this was Saturday and they came to "town."

Fresno, Johnny Cool and Hackett were gathered in one corner. With them was a huge, hulking brute, who was tilting a bottle to his mouth as Bonniwell and Slater entered.

"Billy Burks," said Bonniwell, but did not go up to the group. His eyes had caught sight of a pretty titian-haired girl. He swerved toward her. Slater, watching, saw the girl's eyes light up. Then they were out on the floor, dancing.

Rodebaugh passed, a buxom, flaxen-haired girl in his arms.

Slater drifted over to the group in the corner. Johnny Cool's washed-out blue eyes gleamed. "Better behave yourself, Billy," he said. "There's a Texas bad man here now."

Billy Burks blinked at Slater. "Who? Him?"

"Yep," chortled Johnny. "A rootin', tootin', snortin' bad man. You wanna watch your step round him."

"You never give up, do you, kid?" Slater said calmly. He turned away to the dance floor.

Then his eyes lit up. Susan Orpington and her father were just coming in through the door. Slater sent a quick glance to the dance floor where Bonniwell was still dancing with the red-headed girl. He chuckled and bore down on Susan.

Susan was wearing a blue velvet dress with gold sequins. A new dress.

Orpington grunted as Slater came up. "The way you were going when you left, I thought you'd be in Idaho by now."

"Uh-uh," Slater said. "I ran into Jim Bonniwell."

"Slater," Orpington said, "like to have a talk with you."

"After this dance?"

He held out his hand to Susan. Susan started to shake her head, saw Bonniwell dancing. She changed the shake to a nod, slipped into Slater's arms.

Bonniwell had seen them by now. He guided his partner up to them.

"Hello, Susan," he said. "Mighty pretty dress you're wearing."

"Just an old sack I had around," Susan snapped.

At that moment the orchestra stopped playing. The red-haired girl murmured something to Bonniwell and ran off. Bonniwell stepped over to Susan, took her arm.

"The next one's ours." He scowled at Slater. "I waited, and when you didn't show up I thought——"

"You waited too long." Slater said. "She promised the next dance to me. This was just a piece of a dance."

Bonniwell's eyes were smoldering. "Slater, there's something about you that irritates a man."

"Can't imagine what that could be," Slater said, with mock innocence.

Bonniwell would have carried it further, except that the little orchestra began playing again. Susan danced away with Slater in silence.

They made a complete circuit of the floor, passing Bonniwell on the sidelines. Then Slater said, "Well, go ahead."

"Go ahead—what?"

"Is it real, what's between you and Parker?"

"What do you think?"

"He's well thought of in Beaver Rapids. He's got a big ranch and he's no doubt got a lot of money. A girl could do worse."

"You're a fool, John," Susan said with warmth. "You know that, don't you?"

They were near the entrance and Slater suddenly propelled Susan through the door, took her arm.

"I want to talk to you."

"You could have talked inside—while we were dancing."

"This is a better place."

He led Susan down the short flight of stairs, took her aside, into the gloom of a spreading oak.

"You'd go anywhere with that father of yours. Do anything."

"I told you that in St. Louis."

"This is a dangerous game, Susan. You must have guessed by now that Alan Parker is Jim Bonniwell."

"Is he?"

"Of course he is. And don't be fooled by Bonniwell. The veneer's thin. He's a killer."

"And you? Aren't you looking for a man . . . to kill him?"

He caught her in his arms and kissed her. A violent shudder

134

ran through her body. Then she was pounding him with her small, hard fists. "Let me go!"

He let her go, stepped back.

Bonniwell came down the town-hall steps, stopped six feet away.

"I've been looking for you, Slater," he said. "We're riding."

"Now?"

"Now." Bonniwell made a small gesture to Susan. "Your father will see you home."

She went past them into the hall. Then Johnny Cool came out. He was followed by the others, including Billy Burks. Bonniwell took hold of Slater's arm. His fingers were like steel clamps.

"You're going to get a chance to really show what you've got, Slater."

"A job?" Slater exclaimed.

Bonniwell shrugged.

28

The Big Fork Railroad station was a small, isolated one. The station agent looked through the window and frowned as he saw the man in the linen duster pace back and forth. Passengers were few and far between. Strangers were even rarer. The agent looked at his telegraph key and wondered if he ought to send a message down the line.

While he was debating it, the door opened and the man in the duster entered the station. Behind him swarmed three other men. One had a double-barreled shotgun. All wore linen dusters.

The man with the shotgun said, "This is a holdup. Behave yourself and you won't get hurt."

The station agent looked wistfully at his telegraph key. John Slater crowded past Bonniwell, the man with the shotgun. He grabbed hold of the telegraph key and tore it from the table. In almost the same movement he hurled it through the window.

Bonniwell glowered. "The Limited's due in six minutes," he said to the agent. "Flag her."

"I can't do that," the agent protested. "She ain't supposed to stop here."

"She'll stop tonight."

The agent looked into the twin muzzles of the shotgun and picked up a red lantern. He went outside, followed by the outlaws.

Far up the tracks was a ball of light, the headlight of the train still several miles away. The agent threw his switch. The outlaws deployed themselves, according to a prearranged schedule. Bonniwell gestured to the station agent.

"You can go. If you want to keep all of your skin, you'll stay out of sight."

The rails were already humming from the approach of the Limited. The headlight grew larger and larger, bathed the entire right-of-way in a blaze of white, bright light.

Brakes shrieked and the Limited came to a protesting halt. Fred Rodebaugh and Billy Burks clambered up into the engine, promptly cowed the engineer and his brakeman.

A conductor dropped off the steps of a coach to inquire the reason for the stopping and walked into the hands of Bonniwell and Slater.

"Tell the express messenger to open up," Bonniwell ordered.

The trembling conductor walked up to the door of the express car. He pounded on it with his fist. A rifle slug tore through the wooden door and missed the conductor by two inches. The man dropped to the ground.

Bonniwell pointed the shotgun at the express car door, pulled the trigger.

"Open up!" he thundered. "Open up or we'll blow you open."

The rifle inside barked again, putting another hole in the door. Slater walked forward. "Don't do that, Mister," he yelled. "You're only making us mad. There ain't nobody in twenty miles and you haven't got a chance."

He ducked as a third rifle slug tore through the door. Bonniwell signaled Slater to be quiet for a moment. He remained silent himself for a full thirty seconds.

Then he rapped on the side of the express car. "We've got the dynamite set. I'll count three, then light the fuse. One, two . . ."

"All right," came a muffled shout. "I give up."

"Open the door," Bonniwell ordered. "Open the door and throw out your rifle."

The door squeaked open and a rifle clattered to the right-of-way. Then Bonniwell and Slater clambered into the express car. At the last moment Johnny Cool came out of the darkness and climbed in.

Inside, the group walked to a huge steel safe at one end of the car. There was a light hanging over it and beside it a workbench on which were stacked several small wooden boxes.

Bonniwell pointed to the safe. "Open it."

The messenger swallowed hard. "I—I can't. It's a through safe. They—they open it in San Francisco."

"Don't give me that." Bonniwell snarled. "Open that safe or I'll blow your head." He made a threatening gesture with the shotgun.

Johnny Cool crowded past Bonniwell and smashed the express messenger in the face with the butt of his revolver. Blood spurted from the man's face and he reeled back.

Slater said, "Do that again, kid, and you're a dead man."

"What the hell," Cool snarled.

"I'm backing him, Johnny," Bonniwell snapped. "Anything that's done here, *I'll* do."

The messenger stumbled to the workbench. "Here it is," he babbled, "the proof that I can't open the safe . . ." He scooped up a small envelope. ripped out a sheet of paper.

Bonniwell took the sheet of paper, glanced at it and swore feelingly. "They're getting too damn smart, these train people. Next time I *will* carry dynamite."

"How about the registered mail?" Slater asked.

Bonniwell looked sharply at Slater. "I don't want the United States Army on my trail."

"Then it's the safe," Slater said, "or nothing." There was a short-handled ax lying on the messenger's table. Slater picked it up, went forward to the safe and stuck the sharp edge of the blade in the crack of the safe door. He pried sideward. The blade snapped.

Slater swore and, reversing the ax, smashed at the combination. The ax ricocheted from the hard steel knob and tore from Slater's hand. It flew to the table, embedded itself in one of the small wooden boxes.

Slater went to retrieve the ax—and froze.

Bonniwell's eyes followed Slater's. Then he sprang forward. "Gold!" he cried.

It was true. The ax had splintered the board of one of the boxes and several gold eagles had trickled out. Bonniwell grabbed the ax from Slater's hand, smashed at a second box. Gold coins spewed forth.

There were six boxes altogether. Each contained $10,000 in gold coin.

Twenty miles from Big Fork, Bonniwell halted and divided the gold. Seven men, eight shares. Bonniwell as leader took two shares. There were no protests. It was the accepted custom.

Then the outlaw chief made an announcement. "Boys, this is a big thing. Curtis Bligh's going to be after us. So is just about every marshal and sheriff in the territory. And a few thousand citizens who'll be after the reward. We've got to scatter and hide. Until things cool off."

"I'm for California," Johnny Cool declared. "Winter's coming and I've got a lot of money to spend."

"You'll spend it, all right," Rodebaugh chided. "Then you'll pull something and get yourself hanged."

"Fred's right, Johnny," Bonniwell said. "You can't be trusted alone."

"The hell I can't," Johnny cried. "I don't need a nursemaid."

"I'll go with you, kid," Burks growled.

"And you'll take Fresno, too. The three of you stick together. For six or seven weeks, then you percolate back to the hideout. That's an order." He turned to Hackett and Rodebaugh. "You two go together. Slater, you're not known too well. You come with me."

29

Three days later Slater and Bonniwell rode into a landlocked valley, in which the grass was green and lush. A shallow stream flowed through it. A few hundred yards from the stream was a rubble of burnt. rotting logs.

The two men stopped by the stream to water their horses. While the horses were drinking their fill. Slater looked at the remains of the log cabin and what had once been a stockade enclosing the cabin.

Bonniwell's eyes went uneasily to the heap on which Slater's eyes were focused. "Let's get going, this place gives me the willies."

"How come. Jim?" Slater asked.

"It's something I'd rather not talk about."

"Why not?"

"Because I don't want to!" Bonniwell said testily. Look, Slater, we've been alone together now for three days and I don't mind telling you. you don't wear well."

"Because I danced with Susan Hastings?"

"You're asking for trouble Slater."

"Does she know you're Jim Bonniwell. the outlaw?"

"Slater, I said—" Bonniwell began savagely.

Slater went on harshly, "Although that shouldn't make any difference. Her father's on the dodge himself. She shouldn't mind marrying an outlaw."

Bonniwell's face went white. He jerked on his horse's reins, so that the animal shied back from Slater's.

"Reach for your gun, Slater!" he snarled.

Slater dropped the reins of his own horse, deliberately gripped the pommel of the saddle with both hands. "You can't pick a fight with me, Bonniwell."

"*You* picked it!"

"I merely said the girl shouldn't mind marrying an——"

Bonniwell yelled in rage and spurred his horse forward. The animal leaped up beside Slater's and Bonniwell smashed savagely with his fist at Slater's face. Slater, trying to duck, took the blow on his forehead. He was almost dislodged from his saddle, but recovered and struck back at Bonniwell.

Bonniwell lunged out, caught hold of Slater and both men went into the water, between the horses. The animals promptly shied away, leaving the two men threshing in the creek.

For a moment they clinched in the water, then almost by mutual consent separated. As they parted, Bonniwell hit Slater squarely in the mouth, upsetting him. Slater swallowed a great mouthful of water, came up sputtering. And hitting. Bonniwell went back to the edge of the water, felt land and began clambering out.

Slater followed. To his credit, Bonniwell waited until Slater was on land before attacking. But then his assault was a furious one. Slater took a hard blow on the chin, a right in the stomach that bent him over, then an uppercut that lifted him off his feet and deposited him on the ground on his back.

He rolled over quickly, got to his feet and rushed Bonniwell.

The outlaw chief met Slater with a smashing blow that dropped Slater to his knees. He fell forward and, catching hold of both of Bonniwell's legs, clung to them. Bonniwell tried to shake him off, couldn't, and struck down at Slater's head.

The blow broke Slater's hold. He fell backward, got to his feet once more.

Bonniwell stepped in for the kill. He measured his victim, drew back his fist and swung. Slater saw the blow coming, fell sideward. The fist missed by a fraction of an inch and was delivered with such force that Bonniwell was thrown off balance. Before he could recover, Slater clubbed him savagely on the right ear, followed through with a one-two to Bonniwell's body that left the outlaw gasping.

It was Slater's fight now. He hit Bonniwell again and again, took one or two light blows in return, but kept hammering away until Bonniwell was down on his knees.

By that time Slater's fists were like lead. He stopped and looked down at the panting Bonniwell.

"All right, Bonniwell," he said. "I take it back."

"I won't accept it, Slater." Bonniwell gasped in a great lungful of air. "But you make a good fight."

Slater grinned weakly. "You're not so bad yourself." He helped the outlaw to his feet. "Now, let's talk."

"About what?"

"That place over there, those ruins. You know what they are."

"That's what I tried to tell you before—before the fight. Of course I know what it is. The place they used to call Fort Starvation. My brother was killed there."

"My name is Slater," Slater said grimly. "John Slater."

Bonniwell looked at him puzzled. "Am I supposed to know . . . ?" Then he suddenly gasped in astonishment. "There was a Slater here . . ." He pointed at the ruins of Fort Starvation.

"My father."

"Be damned!" exclaimed Bonniwell. "It's a small world."

"Not so small, Bonniwell. You certainly don't think I threw in with you by accident, do you?"

Bonniwell's eyes narrowed. Then he looked again at Fort Starvation. For a long moment, during which time Slater watched him closely. Finally Bonniwell's eyes returned to Slater.

"All right, talk."

"A group of prospectors wintered there during the winter of 1860-61. They were attacked by Indians and when a detachment of cavalry came along in spring they found five corpses . . . mutilated corpses . . ."

"I know the details," Bonniwell said. "I got them from the Army."

"Then you know that five men were buried there."

"Yes. My brother . . ." Bonniwell shrugged. "Your father, you say, and three others."

"Douglas Carson, George Lake and Axel Turnboom. But I happen to know that *six* men wintered there."

Bonniwell nodded. "I know that, too."

It was Slater's turn to show astonishment. "You knew?"

"My brother wrote me a letter in the fall."

Slater held his breath. "Did he—did he name the man?"

Bonniwell took his time before replying. "Yes."

Slater let out his breath in a rush of air. "What was the name of the sixth man?"

"You don't know?"

Slater grabbed Bonniwell's arm in a savage grip. "Would I be here if I knew?"

Bonniwell jerked his arm free. His voice became harsh. "I don't get the point of all this? What happened here in this valley—well, it happened. And it was a long time ago. There's nothing you can do about it now."

"You fool!" cried Slater. "Don't you understand? That sixth man sold out the others, your brother—my father. He's responsible for their murder. My father—your brother—they starved and they—they did things that a man shouldn't do. And then they died . . . murdered because that sixth man sold them out . . . for sixty thousand dollars in gold."

"All right," said Bonniwell, "but the man's dead——"

"He isn't!" Slater cried. "He's alive today."

Bonniwell backed away. He looked at Slater for a moment, then sat down on the bank of the creek. "My brother wrote me about the gold, said if anything happened to him to dig under the gate of the stockade——"

"Then let's dig!" cried Slater.

Bonniwell laughed shortly. "Don't you think I dug? I came out here in '63. I dug. I dug up all around the place and it was gone. It was a waste of time and I knew it would be, but I dug anyway. The gold was gone."

"Taken by the sixth man—after the massacre!"

Bonniwell shrugged. "What else? People have been murdered for a lot less."

"You're a killer," Slater said savagely. "A life or two doesn't mean a thing. But my father was murdered here in this valley——"

"So was my brother!" snarled Bonniwell. He got to his feet. "I'm fed up with all this rehashing of old stuff, Slater.

143

Your father was killed, so was my brother. For sixty thousand in gold. But the gold's gone."

"Just tell me," Slater pleaded. "Just tell me the name of the man who took it."

"The man's dead. I tell you. It wouldn't mean a thing——"

"I tell you he's alive. I know it."

"How do you know it?"

"Because I was here myself just a few months ago. Some-one had been prying around only a day or two before me and —and while I was here he took a shot at me."

"He didn't kill you? So you saw him . . ."

"Only at a distance."

"It wasn't me, Slater. That's all I can say."

"You can tell me the name of the man. I'll find him."

"I'll tell you nothing, Slater. If he's alive——"

"If he's alive, you'll go after him, is that it? You'll shake him down for whatever he's got."

"This outlaw game's played out. If there's a chance for me to make a big chunk of money, like you say . . . all right, I'll make it. I thought the man died years ago, but if he's still alive, I'll find him. . . ."

"That's your last word, Bonniwell?"

"It is!"

30

In the little Mormon village on the western side of the mountains that encircled Fort Starvation, Bonniwell bought a newspaper. He carried it to Slater.

"Fresno and Burks've been captured!" Bonniwell said tautly.

Slater read quickly through the story. Yes, Burks and Fresno had been taken. With Johnny Cool they had entered a store near Buffalo Grove, just over the Wyoming line. A quartet of cavalrymen from a near-by fort had happened into the store. They were there innocently enough. but Johnny Cool had opened fire on them. The cavalrymen had returned the fire. Burks and Fresno had fallen, wounded. Cool, who had been responsible for the fight. had made his getaway. One soldier had been killed. another wounded.

Slater regarded Bonniwell soberly. "Fresno wasn't a bad sort."

"He was the best. He and Burks haven't got a chance. They found the gold on them and Curtis Bligh won't let up until Fresno and Burks are stretching rope." He came to a sudden decision. "We've got to spring them."

Slater looked at Bonniwell in astonishment. "That's nonsense. They're in Bernie Cassidy's jail and this paper says that Bligh's making his headquarters in Beaver Rapids. He's got twenty men there, just in case you should try anything foolish. . . ."

145

"They won't hang Fresno and Burks. I promised them that long ago. I promised it to all of the boys. If worse comes to worst we'll go down fighting, but none of us will stretch rope."

Colonel Orpington crossed from his cabin to the barn. Before he entered he looked involuntarily over his shoulder.

In the barn he got a pitchfork and began putting hay from a small pile into one of the horse mangers. Bonniwell and Slater stepped out of an adjoining stall.

Colonel Orpington dropped the pitchfork. "Bonniwell—Slater!" His eyes went quickly to the door of the barn. "How'd you two get here?"

"We pulled in this morning. Didn't want to wake you up."

"It's a good thing you didn't. Don't you know that this place is being watched?"

"So's my ranch," Bonniwell said. "I guess they finally put two and two together."

"They know Alan Parker's Jim Bonniwell," Orpington declared. "They didn't get it from Fresno or Burks, but Bligh seemed to know. He went out there———"

"And found enough evidence? All right, they know. That doesn't change things. I promised Fresno and Burks that I'd help them if they ever got in a jam."

"You won't have a chance," Orpington said. "The town's full of detectives. Curtis Bligh's taken over."

"The devil with Bligh!" Bonniwell snapped. "I've got an ace or two up my sleeve. . . ."

Susan Orpington stepped into the barn. "Then you'd better play your aces," she said.

"Sue!" exclaimed Bonniwell. He started quickly toward her, would have taken her into his arms, but Susan avoided him.

Slater laughed harshly. "What's the matter, Jim? Doesn't the lady care for you now that you're on the losing end?"

Bonniwell whirled on Slater, his face a mask of fury. "Slater, you've prodded me too far. I've put up with you until now, but———"

He reacted suddenly, as violently as if he had been struck.

The others heard it, too, the drumming of horses' hoofs. Bonniwell leaped to the door of the barn, looked out. Two hundred yards away coming fast toward the ranch buildings were four horsemen.

146

Bonniwell jerked back into the barn. "We've got to ride for it!"

Smoothly, Slater whipped out his Frontier Model. "There'll be no more riding," he said.

Bonniwell stared at him in amazement. "This is it, Bonniwell," Slater said remorselessly. "Put up your hands."

"So you're a detective, after all," Bonniwell said.

"This is the way it is," Slater said evenly. "No more, no less."

Orpington took a step forward. "Slater," he began.

Slater gestured him aside. "Keep back, Orpington——"

"Orpington!" cried Bonniwell. "I thought your name was Hastings!" His eyes went to Susan's. "You, too?"

Susan winced, moved forward. She collided with her father. For just a fraction of a second Orpington's body acted as a shield between Bonniwell and Slater. The desperate outlaw used that opportunity. He slammed Orpington violently against Slater, upsetting the latter. Then he whirled, sprang for the rear door of the barn. Slater, recovering, ran after him.

But he was too late. His terrible danger gave Bonniwell speed. And outside, a horse stood handy. He vaulted up on its bare back, headed it for the west. By the time Slater got to the edge of the barn, Bonniwell was disappearing into a clump of trees. He put up his gun, returned and entered the barn.

Bernie Cassidy was just coming in by the front door.

"You're too late," Slater said to Cassidy.

31

Slater closed the door of the marshal's office and looked at the two cells. Billy Burks was lying on the cot he had once occupied himself for a few hours. In his old cell beyond, Fresno sat on his bunk, playing a harmonica. It was a mournful tune. He saw Slater standing in the aisle, but continued playing.

After a moment Burks began chanting in a deep voice to Fresno's accompaniment:

> "Oh, my name it is Sam Hall, it is Sam Hall.
>   Oh, my name it is Sam Hall, it is Sam
>   Hall . . .
> And I hate you, I hate you one and all . . .
>   goddamn your eyes!"

" 'The Gallows' Song,' " Slater said aloud.

Burks stopped singing and sat up. "Hello, Detective!"

Slater moved forward. Fresno put down his harmonica, stared at Slater.

"Sorry, old-timer," Slater said.

"What're you sorry about?" Fresno asked. "You got your pay, didn't you?"

"And I hope you choke on it," Burks added venomously.

"Guess *we'll* do the choking, Billy," said Fresno. "Me and you." His eyes were still on Slater. "Shucks, what've I got to complain about? I been an outlaw for thirty years. Guess I got

148

in kind of a rut." He paused, then cackled. "An' there ain't much difference between a rut and a grave, except that one's a mite deeper."

Slater turned and went out of the jail. In the marshal's office, Bernie Cassidy was seated in his swivel chair, trimming his fingernails with a jackknife.

Curtis Bligh was seated on a bench, reading some mail he had just received from Chicago. He looked up.

"You didn't have to go in there, Slater," he growled.

Slater said, "Old Fresno saved my life once. The others would have killed me———"

"He's an outlaw," Bligh snapped. "An outlaw and a murderer."

Slater said evenly, "I can't give you my tin badge, Bligh, because I never had one. But from here on, I'm not working for the Bligh Detective Agency. I'm through."

"All right, you're through," Bligh said. "You don't like me, do you? You don't like the kind of work I do."

"No, I don't."

"That's your privilege. Now, I'm going to tell *you* something. I've been a detective for thirty-five years. I've sent a thousand men to prison—some to the gallows. Somebody had to do it, and I was the man that was best qualified. I'm not boasting about that, I'm merely stating a fact. I'm a good policeman."

"So is Cassidy."

Cassidy sat up straight.

"Maybe nobody wants to be a criminal," Bligh went on. "Or a murderer. But there *are* killers and thieves; there've always been and there always will be. The law of survival demands that the person who steals or kills be punished. 'An eye for an eye.' Well, somebody's got to do it. And it might as well be somebody who is physically and mentally equipped for the job. Myself. Bernie Cassidy. No, not you. You haven't got the heart for it."

"Maybe he ought to lose an eye," Cassidy said. "Then he wouldn't need the heart."

Slater turned, started for the door. Cassidy picked up a long, thick envelope. "Take your mail, Slater. Just came in."

Automatically, Slater turned, took the thick envelope from Cassidy. His eyes went to the printed return address: "Western Department, United States Army, Jefferson Barracks, Missouri," it read. He tore open the envelope, started out of the marshal's office.

Outside the door he stopped, read the first page. It was a letter from Lieutenant Colonel Peoples. It said merely that, according to orders given to him by the commanding general, he was enclosing herewith the service record of Colonel Alfred Orpington, U.S.A. Retired.

The attached sheets contained a detailed record of the Army life of Alfred Orpington, beginning with his appointment to West Point, continuing through to the day he had resigned from the Army in 1866.

Slater started skimming through the pages. On page three he stopped. He stared at the page for a long moment, turned it finally and read on. He finished the report, turned back to page three and read it again carefully. Finally, he put the report back into the envelope and put the envelope into his pocket.

He walked down the street to the Placer Saloon.

Colonel Orpington was standing at the bar, an empty whisky glass in his hand. Slater moved over beside him.

Orpington gave him a quick sideward look. "Will you have a drink?"

The bartender moved over. Slater waved him away. He took the Army report from his pocket. Colonel Orpington glanced at the envelope, as Slater extracted the contents.

"Ah, the Army," he said.

"Your service record. It just came." Slater thumbed through the pages. "You were on leave of absence from May, 1860, to December, 1860."

"That's right," said Colonel Orpington dully.

"It also has a notation here, 'Prospecting.' Where were you prospecting in the summer and fall of 1860?"

"Do you have to ask, Slater?" The colonel's voice became toneless. "You're going to kill me. That's all you've lived for all these years. To hunt me down and kill me. Well, go ahead, get it over with."

"Keep talking."

"Is it going to make any difference? You've won. I tried to head you off, I tried to stop you. I couldn't. I've gone over the same ground you've gone all these months. I tried to cover my trail, get rid of anyone who *might* know the an-

150

swers." He laughed hollowly. "And then you got the answer from my Army service record."

"I think I knew it all the time," Slater said slowly. "You didn't stumble on Fort Starvation by accident. You—you were returning to the scene of your crime, that's all. You wanted to *bury* the results of your treachery."

"Treachery? Yes I guess it was. But it didn't happen just like you think. I didn't sell them out to the Indians. I had nothing to do with that." The colonel bit his lip. "Part of the gold was mine to begin with, one sixth. Only . . . well, I stole it all. Then I ran into the war party. I hid out, saw where they were going. I—I even watched them attack the fort. I suppose I could have gone over the mountain, gotten help from the Mormon settlements. I suppose, too, I could have gone all the way to the Army post and gotten a relief column. I didn't . . . because I wanted the gold all to myself. And the massacre covered up my trail. At least, I thought so. To make sure I led the column there in the spring, buried what we found."

"And the gold?"

Orpington pointed at the Army report in Slater's hands. "It's there, isn't it? From Utah I was transferred to New York. I was on recruiting duty until the fall of '61. I had sixty thousand dollars. I put it into a blockade runner. The ship was sunk on its first trip."

151

32

Johnny Cool and Al Hackett stopped their horses in front of the Beaver Rapids bank. Johnny Cool took a stick of dynamite from under his shirt.

"All set, Al?" he asked and touched a lighted cigarette to the short fuse on the dynamite. He waited a moment, then suddenly hurled the dynamite at the window of the bank.

It was good timing. The dynamite exploded just as it hit the bank window. The bank building rocked to the explosion. A sheet of flame bellied out into the street.

In the rear of the jail Rodebaugh and Jim Bonniwell dismounted and hurried to the barred windows. The face of Fresno appeared.

"Glory be, Jim!" he exclaimed.

"Hold on," Bonniwell said. He twisted a rope end around a bar, knotted it quickly. Rodebaugh was doing the same to the bar on Burk's cell window.

Burks roared, "Gimme a gun!"

Bernie Cassidy, Curtis Bligh and three detectives burst out of the marshal's office, started up the street. Then Cassidy, seeing the horses behind the jail, cried out. The men swerved.

Bonniwell and Rodebaugh put spurs to their horses. The ropes, knotted to the bars, tightened and the bars came free. Fresno and Burks started clambering through the windows.

And then Cassidy and the detectives began firing, Fresno

was caught with one foot through the window, one still inside the jail. He remained in that position . . . dead. Burks never got out at all. He fell back into his cell, a bullet between his eyes.

Then Cassidy went down. He raised himself to one knee and fired at Rodebaugh, who was trying to ride him down. The bullet killed Rodebaugh's horse. Bonniwell's horse screamed from a bullet wound, reared up high on his haunches. Bonniwell slid off the animal's rump, hit the ground and started running.

On the street, Al Hackett and Johnny Cool were having the battle of their lives. Men spewing out of saloons and stores were pouring a withering fire at them. Hackett's horse went down. Hackett hit the ground, rolled over. A man with a short shotgun ducked out from a store front, thrust the shotgun to within ten feet of Hackett's head and fired.

A man popped out of a doorway and fired at Johnny Cool. The kid, sobbing, fell from his mount. Bent low, he started running up the street. Ahead, John Slater came out of the Placer Saloon.

"Slater!" Johnny sobbed.

"This time you've got your gun in your hands," Slater called. "Mine's still in my holster."

Johnny fired once, twice. The first bullet went wild by three feet. The second seared through Slater's left thigh. Then Slater fired. The slug picked up the kid and threw him back on his shoulders. He was dead before he hit the ground.

Slater started limping forward. Jim Bonniwell burst out from behind the jail, skidded his horse to a halt. He saw Slater, slid from his horse.

"Slater!"

"Yes, Bonniwell."

"I'm through," said Bonniwell. "I'm through, but I'm taking you with me."

Alfred Orpington came up behind Slater, running. Bonniwell's face distorted. "You first, Orpington. If it hadn't been for you . . ."

His gun came up, thundered. Slater's gun spoke at almost the same instant. Bonniwell pitched forward to his face. Slater, turning, saw Orpington down on his knees, clutching his chest. Bonniwell's bullet had hit him squarely.

A horse came from across the street. Susan Orpington

bounded from it, rushed forward. She fell to her knees beside her father.

"Dad! Dad!" she cried. "Not now . . . not after all we've been through!"

Orpington raised his face with an effort. He smiled, fell forward.

Slater came, stood over her. After a moment Susan raised her head.

"I didn't shoot him," Slater said.

"I—I know. I saw." She got slowly to her feet, looked down.

People gathered around. Curtis Bligh broke through the fringe, moved forward.

"We got them," he exulted. "We got them all."

"Yes," said Slater. "You got them." He turned, walked away. Men gave way before him.

They were hitching a fresh team of horses to the east stage, when Slater came up. A lone passenger was already inside the coach.

The stage driver nodded to Slater. "Be ready in about two minutes."

Bernie Cassidy came out of the stage office. "Nice day for a trip," he observed.

Slater shrugged. "I guess so."

"You'll be on the train tomorrow night," Cassidy cleared his throat. "Bothers you. don't it? I mean, killing a man."

"I was in the war." Slater said harshly.

"That ain't the same."

"He was a murderer and he would have killed me."

"Colonel Orpington?"

"I wasn't talking about Orpington."

"That's right, you wasn't." Cassidy shot a quick look toward the stagecoach office. "Have a good trip east."

He moved aside and Susan Orpington came out of the stage station. Slater looked at her steadily. She held his gaze.

"We'll be traveling together," she said.

"I know. I was going to go yesterday, then I heard you were leaving today."

She hesitated, then suddenly smiled, a quick, warm smile.

"I'm glad you waited."

She turned to the stage door. He took her hand, started to help her up. With one foot on the step, she turned.

"We've got a long way to go."

He said, "Yes, a long way."

Her hand pressed his tightly and she climbed into the stage. Slater followed.

Bernie Cassidy, watching from the stage station, nodded thoughtfully. And for an instant a smile almost flitted across his face.

———

SPECIAL OFFER: If you enjoyed this book and would like to have our catalog of over 1,400 other Bantam titles, just send your name and address and 50¢ (to help defray postage and handling costs) to: Catalog Department, Bantam Books, Inc., 414 East Golf Rd., Des Plaines, Ill. 60016.

ABOUT THE AUTHOR

FRANK GRUBER started his career as a trade journal editor in the Midwest. Despite his success as one of the most prolific western writers in the world, Mr. Gruber always had a desire to follow a more journalistic career. He was the author of at least fifty books, more than fifty-four motion pictures, at least 350 magazine stories and dozens of television scripts. He created numerous western television serials, notably *Wells Fargo,* and was also known as a mystery writer.